WHERE THE HEROES ARE:
Stories of an Immigrant Family and the
Home Front During WWII

Marti Macke

Stackfreed
Press

For my family.
Thank you for encouraging me to
keep writing, one story at a time.

Prologue

This book is a collection of stories about a family. The parents emigrated to the United States from Central Europe near the turn of the 20th century. It is a celebration of survival in a small steel city during a terrible financial downturn followed by a devastating world war. Some of it is researched fact, but other parts are stories from memory, many fictional but emblematic of important events of the 20th century in the United States.

Gary, Indiana, represents everything good and bad about the extraordinary entrepreneurship of striving immigrants.

Gary, before it became Gary, was a vast expanse of mostly marshy land in the middle of the United States, bordering the southern shore of Lake Michigan. Native Americans made it their home for many hundreds of years, living off the flora and fauna provided by the wide-open spaces. At the turn of the 20th century, hugely wealthy men, mainly from Chicago, built themselves a private club where they could enjoy privacy, hunting, shooting, and each other's company away from the demands of their work.

These "robber barons," as they were dubbed by the press, realizing the potential of Gary's geography and the promise of a burgeoning steel industry, took control of the land for the construction of huge steel mills. They could ship raw materials in and the finished steel out, both overland by rail and through the shipping lanes of Lake Michigan.

Named after Judge Elbert Gary, who was the founding chairman of United States Steel Corporation, Gary became a major steel production center, employing immigrants flocking to the US to improve their lives, Black Americans trekking north to escape the Jim Crow South, women going into the workforce to replace the men who had gone off to war, and Mexicans and Puerto Ricans who had flooded into the big industrial centers also to work in the place of those men. The steel industry became the backbone of the war effort and continued to boom through the late 1940s and 1950s. Across the tracks from those great mills, workers from immigrant families like mine built their homes.

Author's note

This book was written to recall dialogue of the 1940s. It exposes fears and labels used for people who were different, or enemies, during WWII. The labels do not represent my views as the author. Instead, they provide historical context. It is my hope that the labels compel readers to pause and consider the impact of language on others.

Part 1:
When We Were Young

Church Bells on Sunday Morning

Even today, whenever I hear church bells ringing, I'm grateful. They remind me of the end of World War II when I looked at "Papa" Peter, and he looked at "Mama" Katya, and we all knelt down together there on the front porch. And Papa began to pray in old Slavonic, *"Oche nash* ... Our Father who art in heaven." And the bells kept ringing as we prayed, on the porch, in the churches and in our hearts.

Growing up during World War II, I learned not to take simple, everyday things like our church bells for granted. President Roosevelt decreed that no bell would peal until the war ended. I suppose if you'd asked me back then what things I missed most in wartime, I would have told you things like meat, real butter, or enough sugar for Mama to make her apple pie. But looking back on it now, the whole thing was rolled up in the silence on Sunday mornings.

I hadn't thought about it for a long time, but now that they've written all the books about WWII and are showing movies like *Saving Private Ryan,* it hit me about the bells. At the age of seven, "the age of reason" according to the Catholic Church, I'd be pulled out of sleep every Sunday morning by chimes of St. Michael's Byzantine Catholic Church, seconded by alto harmonies from St. Nicholas, the Orthodox Church across the street.

Those bells meant it was a special day. Papa wouldn't go to work at the steel mill. All the stores were closed, even Churlin's Grocery, and Mama would be poking her head in to say get ready for church.

Age seven was a big year. I was in the second grade, and in May, I made
my First Communion. But later, on December 7th, the larger world punched its way into our lives, and not one of us would ever be the same. My sister, MaryAnn, would marry a boy and later confront a man. Papa's daily grind became about more than keeping all of us fed. Year after year, Mama's heart would ache until the war ended. My oldest sister Helen's yearning for romance was rerouted to a railroad trunk line until the war

was over. My third sister, Bettie, turned it into her own war of independence, and she left home. We barely heard from her for years.

And the boys went away to bear the brunt of it all. My brothers Peter Jr. and Johnny and MaryAnn's husband Rick went overseas to fight, and their heavily censored letters covered up the horrors of places like El Alamein, Anzio, and Bastogne. They left home dressed in a noble cause, owned up to their fears, and ended up killing out of fear of being killed.

I learned all these things when I was seven. I didn't know then what I had learned, not for many years to come.

Easter on 13th Avenue, Spring 1941

After a dreary Gary winter, I couldn't wait for the arrival of spring and the Sears Roebuck catalog. Girls in pastel dresses, always with matching hats, smiling from those brightly colored pages meant that before long, Mama would tuck her big shopping bag under her arm, and with my skinny seven-year-old self in tow, we'd head uptown.

As soon as we reached our stop on Broadway, Mama would climb down from the streetcar, dig into her purse for a coin, and tell me to "give it to the man over there." People scurried past the small man who sat in an old coat, drab shirt, and wrinkled pants on the sidewalk with his tin cup on the ground next to him. Others might ignore him, but Mama never did.

First stop: Goldblatt's. Huge, the store took up a city block. Men's and women's clothes on the first floor, and cheaper goods in the "bargain basement." When we didn't find a dress for me, we looked around for an Easter hat for Mama while a mousy woman in a tattered coat lingered nearby; I'd seen her in the store other times. She paused, looking us over steely-eyed, and then wandered away. I wouldn't learn until years later that she was the store detective.

On the way out of the store, we passed the deli where workers in white butchers' aprons pulled long loaves of lunch meat from the refrigerated case or cut slices from enormous wheels of cheese. The smells—meat, pickles, and fresh bread always made my mouth water as we passed by.

No hats, but later, we found Mama some beautiful beads at Woolworth's before heading to Neisner's, another dime store, for lunch. Mama thought the vegetables were fresher there and she always ordered the vegetable plate. I had a grilled cheese sandwich and a chocolate milkshake. Then, with stomachs full, we headed home.

The week before Easter was baking week. With five grown offspring plus Papa, me, and Rick, MaryAnn's boyfriend who was always around, Mama never baked one of anything. She started the bread dough in a clean wash tub, with Papa and brothers Johnny and Peter taking turns "punching" or kneading a really big mound. She divided it up and placed it between freshly laundered sheets under the *perina,* or puffy feather comforter, to let it rise. Another round of kneading, then back snug under the *perina.* Now, she formed loaves of yeast breads, nut rolls, *bubalki* (like Parker House rolls drizzled with honey), and poppyseed rolls.

I made at least a gazillion trips to Churlin's Grocery for eggs, flour, sugar, and other essentials for baking. (I'm sure there's still a path there with my name on it.) Taking the shortcut through the alley, I passed Kresny (the name means uncle in Ukrainian) Churlin's smokehouse, whose vents sent heavenly smells of hickory smoked ham, pork ribs, and sausage into my greedy nostrils. I had always been fascinated by the walk-in meat locker in the store, where slabs of meat hung on thick black hooks. I longed to go inside, but children were not allowed in there. One time, when Kresny opened the door, I spotted the side of a carcass with the leg still attached. He came out hefting a slab of beef and thumped it onto the butcher's block. With a flick of his thick wrist, he carved out a roast and then cut smaller pieces, then fed them into a big grinder in the corner. Turning the long handle, he squished those pieces into hamburger, red blood dripping from the bottom of the machine as he cranked.

On Holy Saturday, Mama and I brought our Easter basket to the foot of the altar at St. Michael's Byzantine Catholic Church. Inside the basket were portions of ham, *hrudka* (homemade egg cheese), smoked sausage, ground beets with horseradish, and brightly colored Easter eggs tucked around a small *pasca,* the round Easter bread. There in the quiet church, Mama and the other ladies laid back their hand-embroidered coverings, and Father Papp said a short prayer, sprinkling the baskets with holy water.

Mama's *pysanky,* Easter eggs decorated in traditional Ukrainian style, were works of art. She dipped the head of a straight pin into hot wax and drew on the boiled egg, creating intricate designs, the kind you see in magazines, onto the shells. Then we dyed the eggs with different colors and ate

4

them on Easter Sunday, always saving the prettiest eggs for last.

Easter morning, we all walked to church together, Mama sporting a rose corsage from either Johnny or Peter (they took turns buying it for her). Hi-E (Helen), MaryAnn, and Bettie each wore a red carnation with a ribbon. Mine was unadorned. St. Michael's bells began to peal as we drew close, very soon joined by the deeper tones of St. Nicholas Orthodox church. Father Papp's sermon was given in Old Slovenian (I understood about every third word), and the full-throated choir sang out the music of Tchaikovsky and Rimsky Korsakov, the two composers I remember. The Mass incorporated a beautiful Byzantine chant, which was sung a capella. The choir, led by our opera-trained cantor, John Kahanic, with a tenor voice as beautiful as a waterfall, sang the chants, and we all followed with the responses. Slavic men, at least the ones at St. Michael's, were proud of their voices, so the congregation and the choir gave lusty renditions of *Christos Voskrez,* Christ is Risen. I sang in the choir all through high school, where the choir director exhorted us to "make the windows shake." There, surrounded by singers young and old, I learned to love sacred music and all that it inspired. And we did make the windows shake!

Later, our family gathered around the kitchen table for Easter brunch. We knelt beside our chairs, and then Papa began to pray in Slovak, a language many Ruthenians (modern-day Ukrainians from the Carpathian Mountain area) spoke. And boy, could Papa pray! "Pop shoulda been a preacher," Peter muttered, but when I giggled, Mama shushed us both with "the look." We ate the blessed food from the basket first, making sure everyone had at least a taste of everything, and finished the meal with pastries and one of Mama's brilliantly colored eggs.

The rest of the holiday was quiet. Mama, Papa, and I would visit Mr. and Mrs. Komanecki—Mama's sister, I found out later—or one of Mama's other friends, Cetka (whose last name I don't remember). I sat in the grape arbor, and Cetka kept encouraging me to eat the grapes, but they were sour, and

I didn't like them at all. Sometimes my godparents, Mr. and Mrs. Ragan, came to visit us, and they were very formal; he wore a suit with a vest, and had a pocket watch on a chain.

Though winter in Gary was dreary, filled with gray skies and snow that turned to gray slush, Easter was the sign that spring was coming. My Easter memories, filled with delicious and beautiful food, wonderful music, and the family all gathered together, are some of my happiest.

Green Sunday

Today was a special holiday, a part of the church calendar that we celebrated each year. It might have coincided with Pentecost, but I'm not really sure. We always called it Green Sunday. I do remember it happened every year, sometime after Easter, and I think of it as another of my favorite memories from childhood.

As soon as the first leaves appeared on the trees, Mama and I would head out to the woods near our house to trim off some small branches to use as decorations. We carried them home in the wicker basket Mama had brought along. We placed a branch or two behind each of the holy pictures in every room of the house. We had a lot of holy pictures! There were pictures of saints, the Holy Family, or scenes from the Bible in every room! That was our art. Once all the branches were settled behind pictures, they created an aroma that filled the house with springtime.

Mama had been baking for weeks, and as soon as the house was decorated, she invited Father Papp to come over and bring his bag of anointing tools. When he arrived, he took out his aspergillum, or holy water sprinkler, put on his alb or stole and went to work. He anointed each room, sprinkling each picture, as he and Mama sang the old Russian hymns that were part of our church ritual. I joined in on the ones I knew. Our little parade went from room to room, lobbing blessings into each room and singing as we walked.

After the whole house was blessed, Mama invited Father to sit with us in the kitchen. We had spent weeks cleaning, so the house was spotless. Mama brought out her pastries. We ate her delicious *rozki, kolachi* (a sweet yeast bread packed with cherry, apricot, or sweet Bakers' Cottage Cheese filling), and a few poppy seed cakes while Mama and Father Papp drank coffee (milk for me) and talked about life in general.

Then, Father put me through his "religion quiz." I went every Saturday to "Russian School" in the church basement, where we had bible study and where I learned to speak and read Russian, starting with the Cyrillic alphabet—the Russian

ABCs. At home, we spoke Mama's native tongue, Lemko, a Ukrainian dialect. Papa's language was Czechoslovakian, so we spoke Slovak, too. But to read Russian means to know the Cyrillic alphabet, used in Eastern European countries. At home, we conversed in Lemko but sang in church in Russian or Old Slovenian, an even older dialect.

Father put me through the Ten Commandments, Commandments of the Church, and a few lives of the saints, then nodded his head and pronounced me fit for another year. I remember the doors remained open and the sweet spring air lingered long after Father was gone.

Soon, I spied Papa taking a shortcut through the alley on his way home from work.

"Papa! I cried. You just missed Father Papp. He came and blessed the house. And we ate *rozki*. We saved some for you!"

At Home in Gary/Radio Days

We lived in a two-story house on 13th Avenue. The house was next to an alley. The alley was paved and clean, and one gate to our yard was at the side, so our yard could be entered from the alley. The yard was enclosed by a pretty white picket fence.

Every Saturday, we turned on the radio and cleaned the house, listening to "Grand Central Station, the crossroads of a million private lives, the gigantic stage on which are played a thousand dramas daily," one of our favorite radio programs. I would clean the living room as long as I could in order to hear the story. As I moved into the bedrooms, I turned the volume louder and louder until Mama threatened to turn the story off. It was a Saturday ritual.

Our house was painted white, and flowers bloomed in the yard. A big oak tree shaded the roomy front porch and blocked the afternoon sun, where I would read poetry and opera librettos to my cat. I discovered opera in the eighth grade when I had exhausted the books available from the local library. Looking for new reading materials, I chanced upon a Wagner opera and soon became engrossed in the story. After that, I searched for one opera after another. I loved the opera, though I had rarely ever heard the music. I still love the grand theater that is opera. And it all started on those wonderful summer afternoons reading on the front porch.

In those days, radio was a big part of our lives. Tuesday night, the family would gather around to hear *Fibber McGee and Molly,* my mother's favorite. Each week, Fibber and Molly would need something from Fibber's closet. When he opened the door, we would hear the sound of everything falling out.

My mother would laugh as though she was hearing that racket for the very first time; she laughed so hard she cried. The radio was filled with mystery stories, too, and I loved those the best. They were so real to me that I remember being afraid to walk into a bank in case it got robbed. Bank holdups were a big part of every mystery.

Sometimes my parents and I would go for a streetcar ride on Sunday afternoons. You could pay your dime and ride to the end of the line, where you got a transfer to another route. You could transfer all over town on your dime and enjoy just riding around. However, I hated it when my father told me to sneak on the back of the streetcar right before it was ready to pull away. My parents would get on at the front and pay while I stood on the sidewalk until the doors were ready to close; then, I stepped on. Often the conductor wouldn't see me, and I would get to ride for free. Because I always felt so guilty, one day, I told my father I wouldn't do that anymore, and we had a real argument. But I won and got on at the front of the car from then on.

Though I liked those afternoons with my parents, once I discovered the mysteries on the radio, I begged to stay home so I could hear *The Shadow*. It always opened with, "Who knows what evil lurks in the minds of men? The Shadow knows!" followed by a loud, snide, and evil laugh. Because I sometimes had nightmares, my mother didn't want me listening to those shows. But, after my parents left, I would close the window blinds and even the drapes so that they couldn't see what I was doing. I quaked and shook listening to *The Shadow* all alone, and every time my parents returned, the sound of their knock made me jump.

Sunday afternoon radio was scary, but after-school radio was exciting. I would rush home to hear *Captain Midnight and the Secret Squadron*. The Captain, like the Shadow, fought evil wherever he found it, but because it was a kids' show, it wasn't nearly as frightening. I loved the Captain so much that I had to buy and drink Ovaltine, as he said it was both delicious and very good for us. But when I finally got my mother to buy it, I thought it was awful. My mother said I had to drink it all because we had spent that money. But, despite the fact that I found Ovaltine a rip-off, I just had to have the Captain's "secret decoder ring" to gain "inside important information about tomorrow's exciting episode." Once I got the ring (my mother gave in again), I could decode the message that appeared at the end of the show, "Tomorrow, the

Captain faces another new and exciting adventure." It was another scam.

Nonetheless, I gave the Captain one more shot and hit pay dirt! The "genuine atomic ring," which could only be seen in total darkness, was a true marvel. When I got it and stepped into the closet, I was astonished. From the center of the ring, rays swirled around me into the darkness like green dervishes. When I sent my mother into the closet with the otherwise perfectly normal looking ring, she was amazed. My father was next. He stayed in the closet a long time, then came out shaking his head in wonder, "Son of a sixty-seven!" he exclaimed. And I knew the atomic ring was a success. The Captain had finally come through!

Sometimes on Sunday afternoons, all the kids in the neighborhood would go to the movies. The Tolleston Theater showed Westerns, and we all paid a quarter for a double feature. My favorite was Hopalong Cassidy because he didn't have any smarmy love scenes like Roy Rogers, and he didn't sing songs when he should have been catching bad guys. Hoppy was a no-nonsense cowboy who chased bad guys around on his horse and went from one adventure to the next. Instead of love scenes, there was comedy from Gabby Hayes, his sidekick and grizzled cook. Everyone in the movie poked fun at Gabby, but all the kids loved him. Hoppy always had good shoot-outs, and we kids would come to the theater with our cap guns so we could help him by shooting at the bad guys, too.

Part 2:
Before the War

Life wasn't perfect in our family. We were poor. Our parents were sent to this country by their parents so they could be safe from war and terrorists. Everyone was trying to fit in and be American. For my brothers and sisters, this meant different things. For me, well, I don't know if I understood fitting in. But I loved my family.

The Wedding Rehearsal

"Mama, I'm home!" Katya heard the front door slam and Mari's thin voice calling from the front room. "I saw the wedding cake, Mama! Sylvia's grandma took me down in the bakery and showed me the little bride and groom she's going to put on top. Are you ready to go to the rehearsal, Mama?"

"In my bedroom," Katya called as she slipped her good dress over her head, her fingers working quickly to fasten the row of pearl buttons down the front. The navy fabric lay easily over her corset forgiving a multitude of sins.

"Get the telephone, would you?"

"Take off your boots," Katya said when Mari handed her the phone. "I don't want snow on the carpet."

"Hello."

"Mama?"

"MaryAnn? Are you at the church?"

"No. I'm calling from the drugstore uptown. I was late coming out of the store after work and missed my streetcar. I have to wait thirty minutes for the next one. I'll be late."

"Mari and I are just going over to the church."

"Is Papa home?"

"No. I'm expecting him any minute."

"He promised he'd be there, Mama. He swore he'd show up sober."

"Everything is going to be fine," Katya said as she massaged the dull ache
that had settled between her eyes again.

"Rick said we should have a small wedding. Maybe he was right."

15

"Nonsense. Your Papa was the one who decided we should do it up right, remember?"

"I hope he doesn't ruin everything."

"He won't. Are you wearing your boots? I worry about you in those high heels. You could slip on the ice."

"I'm wearing boots, Mama."

"Good. We'll see you at church." Katya hurried back to the bedroom, snatched some hairpins and her rat—a long silk tube—from the dresser. She started pinning it into a crown around her head, and then rolled her hair over it, creating a dark, shining halo around her face.

"Papa's late, isn't he?"

"He'll be here. Maybe there was a problem at the steel mill, and he had to stay later." But Katya picked up her rosary from the dresser and held it before putting it in her purse. Where was Peter anyway?

Peter had been against MaryAnn's marrying Rick, telling her that she was too good for him. But Katya knew better. Peter didn't like Rick because Rick had humiliated him the last time they had been together.

"My friend Sylvia wishes she had a big sister so she could be in a wedding too," Mari announced as they went into the front room for their coats. "I told her I have three big sisters. I told her Helen is the oldest, but she's not getting married because nobody asked her."

"Mari!"

"Well, Bettie's only fifteen. If nobody wants to marry Helen, I can't be a flower girl again for a long time."

"Don't forget your scarf, 'Miss Broadcast News'!"

"Sylvia wanted to come tonight, but her grandma said friends can't come to rehearsals."

If Pete Jr. wasn't meeting them at the church, she could have sent him to look for his father, Katya thought.

The snow crunched underfoot as they made their way across the front porch and down the steps. Mari ran ahead, skating in her boots on a patch of ice on the sidewalk.

They rounded the corner to see Anna Churlin of Churlin's Grocery Store, and she poked her marcelled head out the door to intercept them. "Steve says the meat will be just right in time for the reception." Through the store window, they could see Anna's husband, Steve, sitting in his favorite spot on an upturned orange crate in the corner of the store, his arms folded over the butcher's apron covering his great stomach.

"We could smell the meat from the smokehouse as we passed the alley. It smells heavenly." Katya could see the corners of Steve's mouth turn up, though he didn't move another muscle. The old poop loves flattery, she thought, and smiled in spite of herself. Anna drew her head back inside, and Katya and Mari trudged on through the neighborhood.

The February air was crisp. Frost painted the window corners of the houses they passed. The street was quiet, its inhabitants huddling inside, warmed by the burning coal whose smoke puffed in black wisps from brick chimneys above. But now at least there's coal to burn, Katya thought, memories of the hard years of the Depression still fresh.

It had been twelve years since the stock market crash of 1929, but the pain of those years lingered. Back then, cold, desperate people had huddled beside the railroad tracks, scrounging for pieces of coal that might be thrown from the cars when the locomotives braked. The railroad security man didn't attempt to shoo them away but turned his back to let them gather what they could find.

"Does Rick hate Papa?" Mari broke into Katya's thoughts. "Of course not."

"Well, he was mad when Papa said bad things."

"That wasn't your Papa, Mari. That was the whiskey talking."

Peter didn't drink all through the Depression. Oh, there was the rare homemade pint brewed by Frieda, Peter's older brother's wife, and paid for down to the last penny every time. Frieda never gave anything away. Any other day, there was no money for drinking.

Peter and Katya had lost their savings in the great bank failure. Soon afterward, work grew scarce. So, trying to keep six children clothed and fed meant that both of them had struggled and schemed just to provide the essentials.

Peter worked out an agreement with Mr. Sturgill, the big boss at the mill.

In return for two days of work around the Sturgill home without pay, he received two days paid work at the steel mill. From his earnings, they bought some chicks and later ducklings and raised them in the back yard for fresh eggs and meat. Peter fitted out the shed so that the flock would keep warm in winter.

In the spring, they rented a good-sized garden plot, and the family had trudged the mile and a half each way to tend the vegetables. There was no money back then for the streetcar. When Mari was born, they trundled her in a little wagon, alongside the other children, back and forth to the garden. At harvest time, Katya spent long days canning to provide stores for the winter.

It was only years later, with Peter finally back at work full time and the bars reopened after Prohibition, that he took to stopping at Whitey's Pub on his way home from the mill. That's when Katya's real troubles began.

"There's St. Michael's." Mari was pointing at the red brick church ahead. "Look, that's Father Papp coming down the steps."

The old priest saw them and waved but turned and kept on walking toward the small brick house next door that served as the rectory. Hands tucked under his surplice and cassock flapping against his ankles, he bent his bald head low against the wind. "Probably went over to turn on a few lights for us, Mari." Katya heard the creak of the hinges as she pulled open the heavy wooden door of the church and followed Mari's slight form inside. The deserted church was quiet. Dust particles hung in the air, choreographed into hazy relief by the late afternoon sunlight struggling through stained glass windows. The smell of lemon oil let her know the ladies of the Altar Society had polished the pews in readiness for tomorrow's ceremony. Probably what stirred up the dust. Only the vestibule light was on.

"It's freezing in here, Mama."

"That you, Missus?" Rudy, the janitor, shuffled toward them, cap in hand, and was peering at them through milky eyes. "I just got here a bit ago, myself. But Father Papp says don't fire up the boiler till you showed up. No sense heating an empty church. I'll get 'er going right away."

"Thanks, Rudy."

"I'll go with you, Rudy! I've never been in the basement!"

"No!" Katya's stern voice squelched the eager look in Mari's eyes. "Here, help me lay this over the altar." Katya took a cloth from her shopping bag. It wasn't cloth from Goldblatt's, where she usually shopped, but from the expensive department store. "I wanted something special for MaryAnn on her wedding day."

"It's really fancy, Mama." Mari ran her fingers over the tatting at both ends of the fine linen, the pattern Katya had labored over, night after night. Every tiny hemstitch was nearly invisible to the eye.

"Anybody here?" Willie Churlin, a big red-faced man who worked in his parents' grocery store, appeared at the back of the church, a thick white roll of cloth hefted over his shoulder. "I brought the bride's runner. Should I leave it back here, Mrs. Cmar?" Katya hurried over to him. "I'm delivering for Amos," Willie explained, speaking of the florist, as he laid the roll at the back. "His truck broke down."

"Oh dear," Katya frowned. "What about the flowers?"

"I'll bring them in the morning. Somebody'll be here by eight o'clock?"

"Yes," Katya smiled, relieved, and thanked him before letting him go.

"Mama?" MaryAnn poked her head in at the back and was peering inside, Rick right behind her.

"Here comes the bride," Mari sang as she ran over to hug MaryAnn.

The bride-to-be put her arms around Mari as Rick gave her ponytail a teasing yank. "Rick saw me coming out of the drugstore right after I called you."

"I was going to pick her up at Sears, but I was too late. I didn't want my bride freezing out in the cold on our big night. My mother said things at our tavern were under control for the rehearsal dinner, so I could leave. Where's Pete?"

"He's not here yet." Katya couldn't look him in the eye.

"So much for all the grand promises! When Pete said he wouldn't ruin the wedding, I actually believed him!"

MaryAnn took Rick's arm and pulled him aside. As they stood talking in tense, low voices, Katya could feel her anger flare. Still, even in the dim light, MaryAnn's black hair made a striking contrast with her moss-green coat. They made a handsome couple—the tiny girl and the tall, sandy-haired boy with a bashful smile. But there was no smile now.

The others were coming in quickly, members of the wedding party in high spirits, ready to practice for tomorrow morning's ceremony. All the lights in the church were turned on, and they could hear Father Papp rustling about in the vestry.

"Hello, everybody! Am I late? I couldn't get off work any earlier. The snow's really coming down out there!" Katya saw heads turning as Helen tripped down the aisle, shaking out long, thick, auburn waves. Moisture glistened on Helen's faux leopard skin coat and hair, adding a luminous sheen to her complexion. She swept the assembly with a magnanimous smile. Helen looked striking, and she knew it.

"Always the grand entrance," Bettie sniffed, following her sister up the aisle. "Does Helen ever just walk into a room, mother? I don't know why she always parades around like that."

Peter Jr. took off his glasses and was wiping them with his handkerchief. "Jealousy in church, Bettie? It makes your teeth fall out!" Then he stretched his lips tight over his teeth and smirked down at Bettie. "No sense gumming our way through the rehearsal dinner, now, is there?"

Katya couldn't help smiling.

"I don't know why you encourage him like that, Mother. It only makes him behave worse toward me."

20

"He's only teasing, Bettie. Don't be so serious." Peter Jr. gave Bettie a broad smile.

"Here, I'll take your coat. We're actually getting some heat in here." Bettie glared back at him but didn't resist his help.

"Is everyone here?" Father Papp was striding to the front of the altar. He stood peering at them over his glasses. "Can we begin?"

With a start, Katya looked around the church. Rick's parents had come in and were standing in a group with their own family. They smiled and nodded in her direction. Brothers and sisters of the bride and groom were all assembled, and each would have some part in the Wedding Mass.

"We'll start with the order of the procession," the priest was saying, and went on arranging things in a brisk manner. Father glossed over Peter's absence, telling Katya she could fill him in later. "The father's role is simple," he said.

Katya's skin prickled. She thought of all the times she had confided in the old priest about her problems. Over and over, he had counseled patience. Patience and forgiveness. Oh, he made an effort to talk with Peter about his drinking, but nothing ever changed. The priest liked to remind Katya that Peter held a steady job and that he had always provided for his family.

"Patience, Katya," he would say. "We each have our cross to bear."

We'll get through this wedding somehow, she vowed to herself. Even if I have to walk MaryAnn down the aisle myself.

Her mind was darting back and forth. Was Peter sick? Was he drunk? Maybe there was an accident at the steel mill. No. Something simple must have happened to make him late. The priest was right that the father's part was easy, and they could fill Peter in later. Even if he missed the rehearsal, he was bound to get there for dinner.

If only he hadn't stopped off at some bar.

As Katya fretted, she remembered the night MaryAnn got engaged:

On that steamy night last July. Peter was drunk. It wasn't anything new. But this time was worse than the others. He was lying on the floor in the front room cursing them, cursing her and MaryAnn, and Rick, of course, and Mari. Katya hated the girls to see their father like that, but she was mortified it was happening in front of Rick. He'd come to take MaryAnn out on a date. Rick took MaryAnn by the arm and propelled her out the door while Katya, helpless, stood looking down at Peter.

MaryAnn didn't come home until late that night, and when she did, she said she and Rick were getting married. Helen and Bettie kept telling MaryAnn she could do better. They made fun of Rick's grammar and said he dressed like a farmer. He was crazy about MaryAnn, but she'd never seemed the same about him. Still, she had made up her mind. Maybe she discovered all the good things about him from having to defend him all the time. Maybe. But Katya knew MaryAnn would do anything to get out of the house.

Peter at Whitey's Pub

Peter stepped into the dim light of Whitey's Pub, his eyes struggling to focus after the glare of the late afternoon sunshine. He could tell it was Whitey's voice, but he couldn't make him out. Not yet.

"The newspaper says German subs are patrolling up and down the Canadian coast. Wouldn't surprise me if they were patrolling the American coast, as well."

"Afternoon, Pete."

"Afternoon."

Gradually, Peter could make out the backs of working men lined up on bar stools and Whitey behind the bar, running his rag across its surface.

"The usual?" Whitey asked, already reaching a thick arm behind him for whiskey.

"Make it vodka," Peter said. "Best not to upset Katya if she smells my breath. Not tonight, anyway." Whitey slapped a shot glass on the bar.

Peter slid onto an empty stool and raised his glass to the men, and one or two returned his salute. Blending into the conversation at Whitey's was like reaching an arm into his old flannel shirt; there was an easy familiarity about them both.

"Just last week, one of those subs blew up a Canadian ship out of Bedford Basin." The cigar stub clenched between Whitey's teeth jiggled when he talked, and its sweet odor hung in the air. "Getting' too damned close, if you ask me."

"You heard about Eric Bice?" asked one of the men further down.

"What about him?"

"His old man told me he crossed the border into Canada last week. Looking to join the Canadian Air Force."

"That right?"

"He won't be the last young hothead from the area going up to join the Canadian military. If I was younger, I might think about going myself."

"Pat McMannus' sister is married to a Canadian kid who was killed on that ship," Whitey said, sloshing glasses in the sink. "Too close for comfort, is what I think."

Too close is right, Peter thought. Canada, in its role as an independent state of the British Commonwealth, had been at war with the Germans since 1938, standing with England by sending troops to Europe. He thought about his sons. Johnny had a good head on him and wouldn't rush into a fight, but Peter Jr. was a loose cannon, and you could never tell what he might do. And now there was MaryAnn marrying that young fool, Rick. Peter sipped his vodka.

"Stoking up for the big day, Pete? Wedding's not till tomorrow."

"Damned fool time to get married," Peter muttered.

"Was there ever a good time?" Whitey asked. That brought a hearty laugh all the way down the line.

"I tried to tell 'em they should wait." Peter shrugged.

"Doesn't do any good," said the skinny guy next to him. "I tried to tell my Nellie. Now she's stuck at home with two kids and says she should have listened to her old man."

"They never do."

MaryAnn hadn't listened to anything he had to say for a long time, Peter thought. Where was the girl who had climbed onto his lap and asked him so many questions? "What makes rainbows, Papa, and how can carrots grow deep down in the soil like that?" She had been certain back then that he could explain everything. But somewhere along the line, it had all changed. Once the Papa who knew everything, he'd become a stranger who knew nothing at all. And now there was Rick. He'd convinced MaryAnn that their being together was all that mattered. Damned fool!

"I've got the liquor ready in the back room, Pete. I'll have it at the church hall in plenty of time. Should be quite a shindig."

"Katya insisted we do it up right," Peter lied. "You know women." He sipped his vodka and wondered if he'd been too hasty in telling Katya to put on the dog like that, with dinner, drinks, and music. Not that she'd needed any encouragement, but he'd be the one who'd have to come up with the cash.

"You've got some kind of doings tonight, too, haven't you?"

"Rehearsal at the church and dinner at Schmidt's Tavern afterward."

"What do you need to rehearse, Pete? Just hand 'em your bankbook."

Peter laughed with the rest of them, but he didn't really mind. He'd show them all right, show everyone that the smart-aleck punk who'd followed his two older brothers to this country had done all right for himself.

"Big wedding like that is too expensive for my blood. Told my Grace she should elope. Told her I'd buy the ladder."

Peter held up his glass, and Whitey poured him another shot.

"Have you seen Chick lately?" Whitey asked.

"He's bad," Peter said, shifting on his stool. Seeing Chick made him uneasy these days.

He'd made the mistake of telling Katya how bad he looked. She'd been harping at him ever since that he was going to end up the same way.

"You two have been friends a long time, Pete."

"Since I was seventeen. I came from the old country, full of piss and vinegar," Peter said, running a thumb down his glass and settling into the tale. "Believed back then that I could do anything I made up my mind to." In the mirror behind the bar, he could see a couple of men nod. "I was headed for my brother's place in the Midwest. Figured I had just enough money for boat passage and train fare. But the conductor in Indiana didn't see it that way. He asked for more money, and when I told him I didn't have it, he booted me off the train. Didn't bother him that it was moving at the time."

"You get hurt?"

"Tore up my shoulder, but all I kept thinking was I needed to get back on that train. First, I wandered around, trying to figure out where I was. And I kept asking for work so I could get to my brother's place. I asked everywhere—the general store, the saloon, and a couple of boarding houses. I finally spotted an old lady sweeping her porch, and tried to tell her I'd work for food. She ended up siccing her dogs on me."

"They bite?"

"Oh, yeah. So I slept in the woods that night, wolfing down apples I found on a tree at the edge of town. Next morning, I worked my way along the railroad tracks, hoping there might be something farther on down the line.

"Took me a while, but I came to a dirt road lined with tarpaper shacks. At the far end, there was this guy bent over in front of a shack. He was stirring something in an iron kettle hanging over a fire. I can still remember it. I never smelled anything so good. He took me in, let me sleep in the shack and share his food till I found a paying job. We cooked all our meals in that pot hung from a tripod in the mud street. Chick had always said he could hear my stomach growling before he could see me. We worked long hours for seventeen cents an hour; we caroused and drank on weekends. We had great fun back then. He was my lucky charm from the first day I got here. Lucky thing for Chick that I found him, too. I've been the closest thing the old man ever had to a family. Never did get back on that train." Peter finished his vodka and laid his money on the bar.

"Give him my regards," Whitey said.

"Sure." Outside, Peter turned up the street toward the rooming house where Chick lived. He wouldn't stay long. He needed to get back in time for the rehearsal, and seeing Chick so sick was a sad chore every time he went these days.

Peter remembered his shock the first time he'd seen Chick lying there, all swelled up like an oversized balloon. Whitey had gone with him that time. Chick told them his kidneys were failing, and that Doc Wimmer came by to stick him with a needle to drain the fluids that kept filling him up. "Tapped him like a keg," Whitey told people afterward. Whitey never went back after that.

But Peter had an obligation. It was Chick who had befriended him when no one else would. They'd lost touch for a long time. When Chick turned up again, Katya didn't want

26

him coming to the house. "He smells of whiskey, and I don't want him around the girls," she had said. When Peter found the old man was ailing, he started going around to see him.

Peter turned into Chick's street to see the landlady waiting on the porch of his rooming house to intercept him.

"You just missed him. Chick's gone," she said it like he'd just stepped out for an errand. "Doc's still up there. Go on up."

He climbed the stairs. Chick's bloated body covered the single bed. "I couldn't get here sooner," Peter lied.

"Yeah."

"But you were here, Doc. You and the old lady." Doc shrugged. "We barely knew him."

"Was he ... did he ... how was it for him?"

"Well, in a case like his, it's rarely good. He had an envelope for you. Waiting to give it to you himself. Said you were the closest thing he ever had to a son," Doc said. The words cut Peter like a knife. He jammed the envelope in his pocket, his eyes filling up so much that he had a hard time seeing his way back down the stairs.

Peter's hand was numb on the railing. Doc must have guessed he'd stopped off at Whitey's. So, what the hell? How could he know when Chick would cash in? The past week hadn't been any picnic for Peter. His boss was always ragging him, blaming him for all the mistakes everyone made. Had the nerve to tell Peter he was getting to be a danger on the job.

The old lady intercepted him at the bottom of the stairs, asking, "Did you get to see him?"

Peter didn't answer. He pushed past her and stumbled on down the street. Back home, he let himself into an empty house. What time was it, anyway? Well, no matter. It was a relief to find everyone gone. Katya, thin-lipped lately, was always waiting to lay into him as soon as he showed up, and the rest of them weren't any better. Still, he wouldn't mind talking to Katya right now, letting her know what he'd been through. He started to get dressed in the clothes she had laid out for him, but his mind was clamped on Chick, on the swollen body sprawled over the bed, eyes bulging like a dead

27

fish. Wasn't Doc supposed to close his eyes? Isn't that what they were supposed to do?

Peter's hand shook when he reached for his tie.

He went to the dresser and stood working the tie under his collar. Katya had insisted he wear the damned thing tonight. Why did he need a tie, anyway? You'd think MaryAnn was marrying some king or something. He saw the clock on the nightstand and couldn't believe how late it was. He was having trouble trying to figure out the knot. Peter's hands were shaking badly now. He needed something to steady his nerves.

He began to rummage through his dresser, in the bottom drawer, far back where he seemed to remember hiding a pint. He found one, all right, but it was empty. Stuffing it back in the drawer, he hunted through the house, high in the kitchen cupboard and under the front room couch. He headed for the shed out back, groping behind the tools on the far end of the worktable. Nothing. He was starting to panic. Katya must have found his bottles and thrown them away. Damn the woman. And damn the tie that was becoming a noose around his neck. He tugged at the knot. How could he think Katya would sympathize with him, anyway?

Back inside, Peter remembered the attic. He could have hidden a bottle up there. He had! After the fight with Rick! His blood still boiled when he thought about Rick. The young whelp had scolded him for drinking, telling him that he was humiliating his family. He ran up the stairs, ransacking everything until he found it. Unscrewing the cap, he took a good, long swig and another longer one after that. Reassured by the warming fire in his belly, Peter could feel the panic subsiding.

He needed to get going. Katya would be madder than hell by now. He took another long pull on the bottle. Damned woman. She didn't appreciate him. He was just the working jackass who handed her his paycheck every week. Where was the "six-Our Fathered, seven-Hail Katyaed virgin" who'd worshiped him so many years ago? Replaced by the warden nagging that he was going to end up like Chick. Well, he wouldn't. No, sir! He could quit drinking anytime. Peter stood. The ground tilted, but as he closed his eyes to right it, the old man's bug-eyed face popped up. Peter leaned his head back and chugged the rest of the bottle.

Drive Home from the Rehearsal Dinner

After the rehearsal, the wedding party all went to Rick's family's tavern to enjoy a rehearsal dinner. It was a pleasant gathering, but Katya was tired and still upset about Peter.

She rode home next to Peter Jr., grateful he had offered to drive her and Mari home early. She had been only too glad to escape. All evening, she had worked hard to keep things light so as not to ruin the celebration, doing her best to gloss over Peter's absence. Her smile had only faltered when she saw the raw hurt in MaryAnn's eyes. Then she came close to breaking down. She leaned her head against the front seat of the car, relieved now by the darkness, and watched the few feeble lights blinking at her from the houses on the quiet street. At least she didn't have to pretend anymore.

"Why didn't Papa come tonight, Mama?" Mari asked from the back seat. "I don't know, Mari. I'm not sure I know anything anymore." Katya was too tired to keep the defeat from her voice.

Peter Jr. pulled up in front of the house. It was dark inside, and there was still no sign of Peter. Katya felt a tinge of alarm but shrugged it off. He's still pulling my strings, she thought bitterly. How many nights had she lain awake, terrified that he was lying somewhere hurt, needing her help?

"Want me to come in?" her son asked.

"There's no need; he's still out somewhere. That's all." The dull pain started up again and was grating between her eyes. She wondered why she had been foolish enough to count on Peter in the first place.

Peter Jr., used to his father's absences, kissed Katya's cheek and drove off again. He was going back to the bar where the others had stayed on celebrating, enjoying the companionship of Rick's boisterous clan.

Katya followed Mari up the steps and into the house. They made their way into the front room, where Katya switched on the lamp.

"Time for bed, Mari. It's late." Katya went to the closet to hang up their coats.

"I'm not tired, Mama." Mari's eyes were bright when she handed over her coat. She was still keyed up from the evening's excitement.

"You have to sleep, honey. There's another big day tomorrow. What if I make you a cup of warm milk? It would help you sleep."

"Nobody else had to come home," Mari protested.

"When you're older, you can stay up late, too. Go out to the kitchen and make sure there's milk in the refrigerator," she encouraged, "that no one drank it, knowing the milkman comes tomorrow." Mari headed out of the room, and Katya paused, rolling her shoulders to try to ease the tension in her back.

"Mama!" Mari's voice was shrill. "Mama! Mama! Come quick!"

Katya ran into the kitchen and almost stumbled over Peter. He was lying face-down on the floor.

"What's wrong with Papa? Is he hurt? He's not dead, is he?" Mari's face was ashen.

Heart racing, Katya knelt down and put her hand to Peter's neck. His skin was warm to her touch. Gradually, she could feel the slow, steady throbbing in his neck. Then she saw the empty whiskey bottle that had rolled beside the sink.

"Damn you, Peter," she hissed softly. "Damn you."

Katya looked up at Mari. "It's all right, honey. Papa is asleep, that's all." She got up and hugged the little body to herself. "He's going to be fine. You'll see." Brushing wisps of hair from Mari's forehead, Katya led her out of the kitchen and into the bedroom. Taking her time, she helped Mari find her nightgown and got her ready for bed.

When Katya came back into the kitchen, Peter was still sprawled out on the floor. She kicked the empty bottle away and heard it clatter against the wall. Peter grunted and turned on his side, away from her. Irritated at him for ignoring her, she kicked at the soles of his shoes. He rolled again and flopped onto his stomach, limp as a rag doll. Katya could feel her temples begin to throb. Suddenly, the anger she'd been pushing down all night erupted.

"Drunkard!" She kicked at his soles again, harder this time. "Is this why you didn't come tonight? Is it? You just drank yourself into oblivion?"

Peter groaned and covered his head with his hands.

"Where were you? Why didn't you come tonight?" She was peppering him steadily now.

"S'matter? G'won," he mumbled.

"You promised. You promised MaryAnn you'd be there." She was drumming at him, at his hips and backside with short, swift jabs. He pulled his legs up and covered his face with his hands. "I was so ashamed. We all were. I stood there with that damned smile plastered on my face all night. Pretending everything was all right."

Peter dragged himself up on one elbow and looked at her, dazed. Then he crumpled again and sank back into a heap.

"Get up!" She took his arm and yanked at him. She wanted to hit him, to beat him with her fists. Instead, she managed to drag him over to the side of the room. Then, flinging his limp arm back down in disgust, she left him there. She turned out the light and went into her bedroom, carefully closing the door so as not to wake Mari.

Furious, defeated, then furious again, the rage threatening to blow right through the top of her head, she pulled a nightgown out of the drawer and began to unbutton her dress. How had she managed to have six children with that drunken sot? Too agitated to sleep, she shoved the nightgown back inside the drawer and stacked her brassieres into a neat pile. She had kept thinking he'd change. Being a good wife, she had followed the priest's advice. "Patience, Katya," said the single man who told women like her how they ought to live their lives. Never trust a man in a skirt! She laughed bitterly and slammed the drawer hard. What had her patience bought her? A drunk who humiliated them in front of everyone. It made her stomach churn.

She pulled out another drawer, mindlessly folding and refolding her underwear. She should have left him years ago. God knows she'd threatened often enough. But where could a woman like her, a woman with so many children in tow, have earned her own way? She was trapped and very angry. How many years had she tolerated, glossed over, smoothed out, and made nice? How many years had she twisted herself into what she had to be, how she should act, and what she must do? The taste of wasted years was bitter in her mouth. It was her own cowardice that had ambushed her.

Flinging out shoes, house slippers, and her old purse from the closet, she found the belt she'd been looking for last Sunday. She didn't bother to hang it up but tossed it toward the heap. She pushed the clothes aside and looked around on the floor. Dust balls lurked in the corners. She hurried away for the broom to sweep them out.

It was late when she heard the car pull up in front of the house. She turned out the light and kept quiet, hoping everyone would think she was asleep. Maybe they wouldn't go into the kitchen, wouldn't find him. Johnny, especially, would be furious if he saw him there, and there was no sense upsetting MaryAnn all over again. Katya was relieved when she heard them go straight to their bedrooms. Before long, the house was quiet again.

Later that night, she heard sounds from the bathroom. Peter was throwing up. The toilet flushed and then flushed again.

"Mama! Mama!"

"I'm coming." She went in to find Mari sitting bolt upright in her bed. "I'm having bad dreams again, Mama."

"Don't be frightened, Mari. It's all right. You can sleep in my room tonight." Katya turned her back on the sounds from the bathroom and propelled Mari into her own room. She tucked her in and sat with a reassuring hand on her arm until she fell asleep.

Later, Peter crept into the bedroom. Katya sprang up and pushed him back out again. "Get out," she said. Her voice was ice. "Get out and stay out." He didn't say another word but turned and went away. The sight of him, of his pitiful shuffling gait, stirred the coals of her anger again. I wish he was dead. What if she killed him herself? How simple. No more walking on eggs, pretending everything was all right. She could have a normal life. Did she know what that was anymore? Oh, she knew, all right. It was what she kept trying to make the neighbors think they had. It was the ordinary days she spent baking bread or hanging sheets on the line. It was when marriage wasn't a giant mistake, and when she wasn't racked with guilt about what life with a drunk was doing to her children. It was when Peter was sober.

Katya had thrown herself into the wedding preparations. The day was going to make up for the bad times. The wedding was going to celebrate the family and validate her. She'd show everyone that, in spite of everything that had been thrown at her, she had been a good mother. She'd accompanied MaryAnn to adulthood and a new life with Rick. Peter wanted to ruin all that. Well, she wouldn't let him. He'd stepped over the line when he turned his back on their child.

Katya stood massaging the back of her neck with one hand. She was tired, but she knew she couldn't sleep. A hot cup of coffee would restore her, but there was no eating or drinking after midnight, not tonight anyway, or she couldn't go to communion at the Wedding Mass. Restless, she tiptoed into the front room. There was no sign of Peter. Going to the closet, she pulled out her coat and scarf and dressed hurriedly. She found her galoshes, tugged them over her shoes, and then made her way to the door. As she stepped onto the porch, a gust of wind caught the hem of her coat and whipped it against her legs. She gulped in the night air, relishing its sting deep down in her lungs. With her boots crunching over the snow, she made her way down the steps, then realized she'd forgotten gloves. No matter. She shoved her hands in her pockets and kept on going.

It was a dark night, and the moon was only a silver sliver in the sky. A planter's moon is what her brother Mike had always called it. Told her the best time to plant potatoes was under a new moon. A wave of longing swept over her when she thought of Mike. She missed him terribly, even after all these years. It was Mike who'd been her sponsor when she came to this country from Austria. It was only because of him that her parents had let her come at all. Mike had promised to look after her, and he even helped find her a job at the Wellington Hotel.

She'd started out making pastries in the kitchen but worked her way up. One night before a banquet, the sous chef was rushed to the hospital with an appendicitis attack. Katya took over, and the diners were so impressed with the meal that they found the manager and complimented him. From then on, Katya oversaw all the banquets. She could still remember Mike's smile when she told him of her new responsibilities and pay raise and how pleased and proud he'd looked.

If only her brother Mike had lived, things might have been different. After all, she had gotten a good job at the hotel and might have stayed there. And Katya would have had somewhere to turn for support, a place to go when things got bad. If Mike were still alive, she might even have left Peter a long time ago. Mike hadn't been keen on him from the beginning, but she was young and in love. Peter, seven years older and with dark, good looks, was more exciting than any of the other men she knew. Besides, she'd argued, wasn't he a good worker who'd held a steady job at the mill? He'd even saved money and built a house of his own. She was sure all he needed was a good wife to settle him down. Finally, Mike gave in, and they set a wedding date. But not long afterward, Mike fell ill with influenza. Two weeks later, he was dead.

She passed Abrahm's Drug Store, its massive shadow rising threateningly beside her. She quickened her step and hurried by. The dark and brooding bakery loomed up ahead and she crossed the street, seeking the safety of the houses on the other side. The buildings, usually so hospitable by day, were strangers tonight.

Katya took a deep breath and let the frosty air cut through her mood. No sense crying over the past. She couldn't change it anyway. There was only the future. And she knew what she had to do. She went back to the house and crept inside. After hanging up her coat, she went into the kitchen, where the stale smell of vomit hung in the air. She turned on the light and looked down at the floor. Peter had tried to clean up after himself, but it was a poor job. Furious all over again, she went looking for him. She finally found him huddled in the basement near the stove, asleep, his head in his folded arms, snoring softly.

"Get up!" She was poking him hard. "Wha…what?

"Get up," she commanded, pushing and prodding him until his eyes opened. Relentless, still prodding, she propelled him half asleep into the kitchen, where she found a rag under the sink and shoved it at him.

"Clean it up," she commanded. "You made this mess. Clean it up before everyone else sees what you've done."

Chastened, Peter did as he was told. He reached under the sink for the bleach, poured some on the rag, and dashed it with water. He began wiping the floor.

Katya cracked the window above the sink to bring in fresh air. She waited until he was finished before she came at him again. "Where were you last night?"

"Katya, I'm sorry about what happened."

"Why didn't you come?" she demanded, keeping her voice low so as not to wake the others. They couldn't start the wedding day with a shouting match. "We were all waiting for you. I kept looking around. Making up one excuse after another. You promised MaryAnn you'd be there."

"I was on my way. I really was." He wiped an arm across his forehead. He looked miserable. She didn't care.

"Chick's dead, Katya. He died yesterday afternoon. I got there too late. When I came home and saw I was late for MaryAnn's dinner, I just needed a bracer, that's all."

"A bracer?" She grabbed the empty bottle and held it up. "You call this a bracer? What about the wedding rehearsal?"

"I was planning to come, Katya. I really was." He was pleading now. "I couldn't even get my goddam tie on."

"Why didn't you come to the dinner late? Tell us what happened? Let us comfort you?"

"I was going to come. It just didn't turn out the way it was supposed to, that's all."

"Look, Peter—I'm sorry about Chick. I really am. But he was an alcoholic, and you've known for a long time his liver would finally give out. How else did you think it would turn out?"

"For Christ's sake, Katya, let me alone, will you?"

"No. Your friend died, so you forgot about us and crawled in this bottle to hide. You had an obligation to MaryAnn. How many years has she been waiting for you to be a father? How many damned years have I been covering up for you? Well, it's over."

"Come on, Katya ..."

"Not this time, Peter. This time you pay attention to me. If you don't stay sober tomorrow, and I mean cold sober all day long, I'll leave you. I'll leave you for good."

Then she turned and stormed out of the room.

The Wedding

The next morning, Peter stood in the vestibule of St. Michael's church, trying every way he knew to hold himself together. He had taken two Alka-Seltzers and three aspirins, and Katya had made him toast and coffee. The pounding headache was down to a dull ache now, with bouts of nausea alternating with cold sweats. Still, all of it was tolerable, and by sheer willpower, he knew he could get by.

Everyone else was scurrying around, seeming to have an important part in the wedding preparations. Nobody paid attention to him, which, considering the way he felt, was just fine. The worst thing was the smell of the cleaning fluid Katya had used on his pants. It made him want to gag. And his shirt was too small. His face must be red as a goddamned beet by now. Katya might have given him one of Pete Jr.'s shirts on purpose. He wouldn't put it past her. He drew his watch out of his pocket and saw it was twenty till ten. His hand was shaking badly.

The church was starting to fill up. Old man Abrams came in by himself and took a seat at the back. Must have left that string bean kid of his to run the drugstore for a few hours. Peter's brother Alex was up there, too, with his wife, Frieda. Frank wasn't coming, of course. He had moved to Pennsylvania years ago, and their only contact now was the annual Christmas card. The three brothers weren't close anymore, not like when they were young. Being the youngest, Peter had been the wildest in those days. He felt obliged; it was his way of trying to be an equal in both their eyes. They'd been some trio back then, drinking and brawling their way through the town. When Alex married Frieda, they toned it down some, but not all that much. But when Peter got married, things changed abruptly. Katya didn't take to all the drinking early on. At Johnny's christening party, she threw his brothers out of the house. Frieda especially took offense, and Alex and Frieda didn't speak to them for a long time afterward. The last few years, everyone was civil, but that was all. Katya had cut him off from his brothers. Peter felt sad and lonely. He could use a drink.

"Hold still, Papa. I need to pin your flower on." Helen was putting a carnation in his lapel. The smell made him queasy. Peter didn't go to funerals because he couldn't stand the smell of flowers. He always sat in the last row at weddings, too. Yes, this should be quite a morning.

"Time to move into the church," MaryAnn said, not looking at him, and he followed her inside.

"Look, MaryAnn, I wanted to explain to you about last night—"

"Not now, Papa. There's no time. Besides, Mama already told me what happened. I'm sorry Chick passed away."

Peter breathed a sigh of relief. It was easier than he thought it would be. Katya had smoothed the way for him. He looked at MaryAnn, who stood beside him in the long white satin wedding gown. Skinny little thing, not like her mother at all. But he had to admit she looked good. Her dress was plain, not all gussied up like some of them wore, and it suited her. She carried a prayer book with a single orchid on top. He wanted to tell her that she looked good today, really good, but he felt awkward, so he kept his mouth shut. It was hard enough walking the first child in the family to get married down the aisle.

The organ music began, and the wedding procession started up the aisle toward the priest waiting at the altar. Rick's mother, the very large Old Lady Schmidt, marched right by him, hissing pointedly, "We missed you at the rehearsal."

"Nice to see you too," he muttered, but he could feel the back of his neck get hot with embarrassment.

Katya, in her best dress, stepped up beside him, paused, looked him over critically, and seemed satisfied. Mr. and Mrs. Komeneki, the Starost and Starosta, translation: "the old wise ones," smiled at Peter. In old country tradition, they were to act like godparents to the newlyweds, offering guidance and sage counsel if needed. They were dressed in formal attire. Mr. Komeneki wore a tuxedo, and Mrs. Komeneki a long burgundy velvet gown. Longtime friends of Peter and Katya, they were a good choice for the "old wise ones." They would support MaryAnn and Rick in their marriage.

Johnny, sporting a black tuxedo, started up after his mother and Mr. and Mrs. Komeneki. He had one of the Schmidt girls on his arm. She had a big ass like her mother, Peter reflected with perverse satisfaction. Helen didn't seem to mind her partner who was tripping over himself because he couldn't take his eyes off her. Bettie looked awkward beside another brother, and then Peter Jr. with some little blond thing Peter couldn't remember seeing before. There was even Mari, planted next to a boy who stood as rigid as a spike. The kid looked ready to bolt. Some woman, must be the kid's mother, laid a satin pillow in his hand and pushed both kids forward. My God, did it take all these people just to get married?

That same woman pulled MaryAnn's veil down in front of her face. MaryAnn took her father's arm, and they went up. Rick was at the altar, waiting. Once there, Peter folded MaryAnn's veil back as instructed, hoping his unsteadiness wasn't giving the neighbors too much to talk about.

"Who gives this woman in marriage?"

"I do." Peter croaked. Then, giving MaryAnn a stiff kiss, he turned her over to Rick and returned his scowl. Peter tried to smile at Katya when he slipped beside her into the front pew, but she wouldn't look at him. God, he needed a drink. Father Papp began swinging the incense everywhere, and Peter gripped the pew in front of him; gripped it until his knuckles whitened. That night at the reception in the church hall, Peter threaded his way past long tables covered with white tablecloths. Places were set for the chicken dinners the church women were finishing up in the kitchen. In addition, there would be ham and sausage from old man Churlin's smokehouse.

Women from church volunteered to cook for special occasions like this. That meant the cost of the dinners was low, and the modest profit was socked away for Father Papp's dream of a new church. Katya told him that the musicians would cost as much as the food, and liquor would be their biggest expense. Rick didn't want any booze, but Peter had insisted. No way was he going to have people calling him a cheapskate behind his back.

He went over to the bar, a long table lined with liquor bottles. Johnny poured him straight seltzer, glowering as he handed it over. Katya must have told him about last night because he'd been hanging around Peter all day, saying little, just watching him like a hawk. He could barely pee on his own.

If he'd had more time, he could have squirreled a bottle into the toilet tank here at the hall. He smiled remembering all the other times he'd outsmarted them. Mostly it hadn't been that hard, and he found himself enjoying the game. He looked over at MaryAnn and Rick, surrounded by well-wishers. Rick looked back and frowned. Nice. Really nice.

He took a long pull of the seltzer and headed across the room to distance himself from the bar. He made a face. How did people drink this stuff anyway? He looked around for Katya. She was bound to have more aspirin in her purse. "Well, Katya managed to put on quite a show this morning. She ought to be happy," Frieda said as she intercepted him, a tiny smile etched on her ferret face. His brother Alex, his stomach hidden inside his size forty-four jacket, planted himself alongside her.

"Looks like you could use a drink, Pete."

"I'm taking it easy tonight. Boss's orders." No sense lying. Alex could always tell when Peter had the shakes.

"Katya's got you trained, hasn't she?" Frieda loved to gloat.

"No question about that, Frieda. But the bar's open. You two go on over and help yourselves."

All night long, people kept coming up to talk, but Peter had trouble concentrating. The music was making him jittery. He downed one glass of seltzer after another, clutching each glass to steady himself. He found himself hanging onto everything—silverware, a table edge. Finally, he shoved his hands into his pockets and balled them into fists, squeezing until his fingers were numb. That's how he got through the night. But he kept his promise.

41

When they came home, Peter was restless, but he went to bed, anyway, and finally fell asleep. Memories of Chick's swollen body kept hounding him all night, and he woke tired. The next day was Sunday, and the day dragged on forever. That night was even worse. He woke early and went downstairs to stoke the furnace. He stayed awake until the alarm went off, then left for work ahead of time. He put in a full shift.

Three nights later, Katya brought the clock up close and saw it was midnight. Peter hadn't come home. She had been lying wide awake in bed for an hour. She had really believed things were working out this time. Peter hadn't touched a drop of liquor at the wedding. Now, here she was, right back where she'd started. But this time, Peter could rot out there for all she cared, for she had made her plans. She got up and began pulling her things out of the dresser drawer, stacking them on top. She wanted to go in and gather up Mari's things, too, but didn't want to wake her. So she tidied up the bedroom a bit and then crawled back into bed. This time, she fell into a sound sleep.

"Mama!"

Katya woke with a start. What was that noise? "Mama!"

Mari's voice rose above a heavier, more threatening sound. Pounding. Something was pounding in Katya's head. Gradually, she came to her senses. The racket was coming from the front of the house. Someone was beating on the door.

"Mama? Are you there?"

"I'm here, Mari. It's all right, honey. Just stay in bed. Someone is knocking at the door, that's all."

Katya grabbed her robe and ran barefoot into the front room. Johnny was right behind her. The rapping on the storm door was so loud it was making her heart thump. A red light flashed on and off in the room, throwing a crazy quilt over the furniture. Katya fumbled with the key in the lock and managed to open the door.

"Police! Open up."

Two burly policemen stood on the front porch holding another smaller man between them. It was Peter.

"Sorry to wake you like this, missus. But we got a complaint about a disturbance at the cemetery. We went out to find the suspect here trying to attack two boys. He claims this is where he lives."

Katya could barely find her voice. "What happened?" Peter had a puffed lip. He struggled to get free, but he was no match for the men on either side. "Is he all right?"

"He'll be fine, ma'am. Just a little worse for wear."

"What was he doing in the cemetery?" Katya heard the disgust in Johnny's voice as he arrived in the living room.

"Two young couples were parked out there. One young lady thought she saw something moving outside in the dark. One of the boys picked up a tire iron, and they crept out to see what was going on. They found the suspect apparently asleep on top of one of the graves. They could smell the drink on him. They tried to get him up, but he got belligerent and came at them. The caretaker heard the commotion and came running. He's the one that called the station."

"Is he under arrest?"

"No ma'am. The boys talked it over and agreed not to file charges. Lucky they found him, too. Cold as it is tonight, he could have frozen to death."

"Yeah. Too bad," Johnny spat. Peter Jr. beside him now looked stunned. "He's in pretty bad shape, but we finally got his address out of him so we could bring him home."

"He doesn't live here." Out of the corner of her eye, Katya could see her girls. The sight gave her courage.

"You saying this isn't your husband, ma'am?"

"Yes, he is, but I don't want him in the house." Her bare feet were freezing. "Charge him with something. Anything. Just take him away."

"Katya … wassa …." Peter's eyes finally focused; she could tell he was furious at her.

"Drunk and disorderly, eh?"

"Hellsa matter wi' you …?" Peter was flailing around.

"Just get him away. My little girl is only seven."

43

The one cop grabbed Peter roughly. "Okay, buddy, that's all for you. We're taking you downtown. We'll see how you like it there."

And they led him away.

The next morning, Katya did the bravest thing she'd ever done in her life. She changed all the locks. The man from the hardware came out first thing. She wouldn't be driven from her home. If anyone was going to leave, it would be him.

She went downtown the next day to press charges, but she took her time about going to see Peter. When she did, she could see he was in bad shape. She went back the following day, and they talked. Peter had gone to the cemetery to find Chick, to tell him he was sorry. It was dark and he tripped over one of the stones, he didn't know which one and must have hit his head. That's where he split his lip. He couldn't remember much after that. Katya listened and then laid her demands on the table. She said she'd be back the next day for his answer. When she arrived, Peter told her to get ahold of Doc Wimmer. Peter was ready to get help. But his promises didn't last, and Katya had to take action. She needed to leave.

Benton Harbor

There was a suitcase by the front door. Mama came in from the front bedroom dressed in her winter coat and dress boots. "I have to go now. Listen to MaryAnn, Mari, and do what she tells you." She gave Mari a distracted hug and headed for the door.

"Mama, where are you going?"

"Everything will be all right, Mari. Just listen to MaryAnn."

"Mama, are you all right?" What Mari meant was, would they all be all right without Mama? "Where are you going? When will you come back?"

"I have to go, or I'll miss my streetcar." Mama checked her watch and picked up the suitcase before opening the door and stepping outside. Mari was frightened. She had never seen Mama like this. The door closed with a snap and the house was suddenly very quiet.

"Where did she go?" Mari asked.

"To Benton Harbor," MaryAnn answered.

"Where's that?"

"In Michigan."

"Why?"

"To the mineral baths. She's going to a spa."

"What's a spa?"

"It's a place people go to get treatment—medical treatment."

"Why does she need medical treatment?"

"Because she's mad at Papa."

"Because he drinks," Mari finished for her. "This morning, they were arguing in the kitchen again. It woke me up, and then Mama shushed Papa the way she always does. Will she come back?"

"Of course, she'll come back!"

But suddenly, Mari wasn't sure. Last Sunday, she and Mama went to hide in Mrs. Oresik's attic after another fight because Papa was drinking. Papa kept walking around outside, calling for them. After a long time, he finally got tired and left.

The house was quiet for the rest of the day. Mari did her homework and played with her paper dolls. Everyone else was gone. MaryAnn made canned tomato soup and toasted cheese sandwiches for supper, and Mari and MaryAnn went to bed early.

The next morning, Papa was banging around in the basement, stoking the furnace the way he always did. The radiator made a few noises, telling them it was coming to life. But everything else was different. There was no blip-blip sound of coffee perking in the kitchen and no smell of bacon to call her to the table. Mari usually ate oatmeal for breakfast, but the smell of bacon had let her know the others were already stirring.

"Eat toast," Papa said, indicating six slices of cold buttered toast in the center of the table. No matter how many times they asked him to let them make their own toast, he insisted on making a pile himself, upset later when no one wanted to eat his cold toast.

Everyone was gone. Peter Jr., then a milkman at Bowman Dairy, left every morning at the crack of dawn. Papa caught the early trolley for the steel mill, and Johnny drove his coupe to the Steel Dispatch Company yard and climbed into a company truck to deliver parts to smaller companies in the area. Helen left for the sock factory, and Bettie tucked her English assignment under her arm and headed across town for Horace Mann High school.

"Bettie will be here when you get home from school," MaryAnn promised. "I'll be home when Sears closes. Oh, and there's peanut butter and jelly for a sandwich after school, and fruit for a snack. And Peter Jr. said he'd save you some chocolate milk from his route." Mari liked when Peter brought chocolate milk for a treat. She often totaled up the receipts for his customers in his book. He checked her arithmetic and mostly said she did good work. It made her proud. "It's like a real job," she said.

The rest of the week passed quietly. There was no word from Mama. Papa was like a ghost around the house. He came home from work and went out to work in his shed, always puttering around, fixing something or working down in the basement. They took turns making supper, mostly lots of soup which they ate with baloney sandwiches. Sometimes after supper, MaryAnn and Rick might go for a drive.

Mari wanted to go for a drive, too. When Mama was home, one of the boys would sometimes take them, Mama, Papa, and Mari, out into the countryside in Portage, Indiana, to "Seven Dollar to get the water." Mama was a big believer in natural therapeutic remedies like waters from the natural springs at the shrine, which came from her memory of springs in the old country. "Seven Dollar" was actually the Shrine of the Seven Dolors or Seven Sorrows on the road to Calvary. Mari hoped the mineral springs were helping Mama. She wished Papa could drive and bring her home. "When is she coming home?" Mari asked every day.

"I don't know. We haven't heard anything," MaryAnn said.

That went on day after day. Mari became more and more sad. After two weeks, on a Thursday, there was a commotion out on the porch, voices chattering and feet stomping. "Here, I'll take your suitcase." Johnny held the door open, and who should come in but Mama with Papa right behind her!

Mari flew into the arms of a beaming Mama. "Are you home, Mama? Are you really home?"

"Yes, Mari. I'm home."

Mari noticed Mama's skin looked a rosy pink, and the lines around her eyes were softer. She realized she didn't look as tired as she had when she'd left.

The next morning, Mari woke to the sound of coffee perking. The smell of bacon warmed the air. She washed her face and brushed her teeth, ready to jump into her clothes even before Mama called her. She couldn't wait to tell her teacher, Mrs. Martin, that Mama had come home! Today was going to be a good day!

MaryAnn's Hope Chest

"Anybody home?" Katya called, knocking at the door of the tiny white house before opening it just a crack.

"I'm in here, Mama! Come in."

Katya stepped inside, slipped off her boots and coat, and made her way toward the voice in the bedroom. She found MaryAnn sitting on the floor beside a long, low chest of highly polished oak, MaryAnn's hope chest. The lid was open to reveal the cedar interior.

"I'm making Rick's birthday dinner tonight." MaryAnn bubbled. "It's tomorrow, actually, but he'll be working late, so we'll celebrate tonight."

"For Rick." Katya smiled and handed MaryAnn a package wrapped in masculine paper. "I found a nice shirt at Goldblatt's."

"If it's from you, he'll love it," MaryAnn said to her mother and laid the package on the dresser. She took two cups and saucers from the chest and handed them to Katya. Then she brought out a small, starched tablecloth which smelled of cedar.

"I still keep my nice things in here," MaryAnn said of Rick's handsome engagement present. Katya knew it had taken MaryAnn a year to collect the things stored in the chest: good dishes, embroidered napkins and tablecloths, her best sheets with the pillowcases Katya herself had embroidered, along with "company" towels and china candlesticks. Closing the lid, MaryAnn led the way into the kitchen. "Not much room in here," she sighed, placing the dishes on the counter and spreading the cloth on the postage- stamp table.

"A doll's house," Katya answered. "You were lucky to find a house at all."

"And one we could afford to rent," she said. Katya knew Rick had taken a job at the factory and was putting in twelve-hour days to save up for a home of their own. Katya's reservations about MaryAnn's marriage had disappeared quickly when she saw how happy she was. Even Peter had to admit it was a good match.

"How's Papa?" MaryAnn asked.

"Good," she replied. "I left him full of my Sunday chicken dinner and reading the newspaper."

"And Mari?"

"Playing paper dolls with Sylvia in the bedroom. Should I make a little coffee?"

"Sounds good. Rick went to visit his brother. He'll be a while."

On her way to the kitchen, Katya remembered the story of how she had started her life in America, just as Rick and MaryAnn were now starting their new life in this little house.

She had been glowing the day she boarded the Lapland ship for her journey to America. She ran up the gangplank, her heart banging in her chest, and hurried to the side to find her parents smiling back solemnly under a cloudless sky. That day, that golden day, she didn't know she would never see them again, for she was young, adventurous, and going to live with her brother Mike in America.

The voyage was a nightmare, a miasma of dank quarters, rough waters, and passengers retching non-stop. A metal gate and a husky crewman barred her way when she tried to climb to an upper deck for fresh air. When she protested, he merely shrugged, and Katya thought if she survived the journey, she could survive anything.

"Why did Papa send me by lowest class?" Mama's frugality, of course. Mama didn't want her traveling to America. "It isn't as though she could be grabbed up into the army," Mama had argued, "she should stay home with us." Katya barely heard her Papa's response that the politics of Europe were changing. What did Katya care about politics? It was America she wanted to see. And when her brother Mike offered to sponsor her in the new land, the decision was made. A woman from their village was making the trip to America. She offered to look after Katya along the way, though she scarcely paid attention to her the whole time they were at sea.

But Katya wouldn't let anything discourage her—not the rough passage, the rancid food, or the long lines they were herded into like cattle when they docked. For when Katya saw

49

the Lady in the Harbor, she was spellbound, heartened that it was a woman who welcomed them. Katya loved the serene face and the strong arm holding the torch, the light for her own entrance into this shining new land.

Katya smiled, remembering how filled with hope she had been that day, and how she had hoped to see her parents again. She reached into the cupboard for the can of Maxwell House and, filling the pot with tap water, she heaped spoons of coffee into the little basket before placing the pot on the stove to boil. "I think I found Mari's Christmas present at the store last week, Mama. A big doll with dark curls and eyes that close. She'd love it."

"You could put it on layaway."

"And get my Sears discount," MaryAnn added.

MaryAnn had insisted on staying on at Sears to help save for a house. She only made twelve dollars and fifty cents per week to Rick's thirty-six, but Katya had to admit her ten percent discount did come in handy. Because married women were routinely laid off in any job, MaryAnn didn't hold out much hope of keeping hers. But her boss agreed to let her stay on temporarily since he was shorthanded.

"I'll get Mari some socks and underwear," Katya mused. "An orange, of course, and hard candy for her stocking. This would be her last year for Santa Claus. Sometimes I wonder if she still believes."

"I think so, but it won't be long, Mama. Mari's growing up."

MaryAnn poured the coffee and pulled some pineapple upside-down cake out of the ice box. They sat sipping from the floral cups as Katya admired the cake on the fancy plates.

"Hand-decorated linens and beautiful china. Just like a fine hotel," she said, enjoying the flush of pleasure on MaryAnn's cheeks. Katya raised the cup to her lips and inhaled the rich aroma. She took another long, slow breath. *I can breathe deeply for the first time in years,* she mused to herself. *I don't have to hold my breath any longer.*

"Papa's quit drinking, MaryAnn," Katya confided. "I know it for sure now. Ever since I went to Benton Harbor, he's been true to his word."

"It's all your prayers, Mama. It's all those candles you lit in church. And the novenas."

"It's a miracle," Katya said.

"But he seems awfully moody sometimes."

"The moods I can take," Katya replied. "Dark moods are better than the terrible binges of the past. And when Papa gets cranky, he goes outside. He spent the past spring and summer outdoors working around the house."

"Well, I have to admit the place has never looked better," MaryAnn agreed. "And Mari. She sleeps through the night. Her face isn't drawn anymore."

"I'm glad to see you so happy, Mama." MaryAnn said, taking her hand. "You deserve it. And I'm really, really glad." Katya felt her eyes moisten, and she looked away. As soon as MaryAnn sensed her discomfort, she hurried on. "I just hope we get snow for Christmas, Mama. It really gets me in the holiday spirit. We'd better start making our plans right away." Soon, Katya and MaryAnn found themselves laying out the events. Katya would have the traditional candlelight dinner for the whole family on Christmas Eve, and later, they would all go to Midnight Mass.

"I want everyone to come over for cake and coffee on Christmas day," MaryAnn said. "It will be tight," she added, gazing at the small rooms, "but I'd like to have everyone at my house, too."

"Where did the time go?" Katya exclaimed later. "I'd better leave you to your dinner. Just a cold supper at our house tonight."

She stepped back out into the brisk air and found the late afternoon sun was already beginning to rouge the winter sky. She walked quickly because she hadn't realized it was so late. Down the block, she saw a figure mincing toward her. She recognized Frieda, Peter's brother's wife.

"Katya! I thought that was you. I've been visiting my son. He got his wife a new fur coat, and they couldn't wait for me to see it!" She lowered her voice confidentially. "It must be very expensive."

"That's nice, Frieda."

"Have you seen MaryAnn?"

Katya gave a brief nod.

"So, how's she doing, married and all?"

"Fine," Katya purred. "Still a size seven."

Frieda's eyes narrowed, but she didn't respond. Katya had been waiting a long time for just this moment. Ever since the wedding, Frieda had been telling everyone that her niece would probably deliver a bundle before her nine months were up.

Frieda didn't have much to say from then on and muttered a stiff goodbye.

Katya crunched on through the snow and was nearing the house when she saw three stray dogs yapping at a ragged shape across the street. *Beggar?* Katya thought to herself. *I haven't seen a beggar on our street in a long time.*

Suddenly, the figure turned and headed toward her. "Is that you, Katya?" Katya saw a thin face peering through a pile of dark hair.

"Why Edith! I didn't recognize you!" Katya said, taking in the baggy sweater hanging underneath the weathered corduroy jacket of her neighbor. Edith Fleming left her house rarely and her appearance was always startling. Her hair poked out in thick, shiny corkscrews from beneath the maroon stocking cap. She stared at Katya intently, her nearsighted pupils enormous and unblinking behind the round steel-rimmed glasses.

"The world is in chaos, Katya. I'm so upset that I had to get out and walk." Katya nodded, thinking that Edith started every conversation without preamble. "We're going to war, Katya. It's imminent. Everyone knows. *The Chicago Tribune, The New York Times*—they're predicting it's just a matter of time."

Edith's intensity always made Katya uncomfortable. She'd been trying so hard to keep the world news from getting her down. It was the Christmas season, after all.

"I think of the families, Katya. Of your family. You have those boys."

"I hope," Katya replied steadily, "President Roosevelt is right. He says we'll supply the nations who are fighting overseas. I hope we, ourselves, can stay out of a war."

"It's only a matter of time," Edith muttered and turned down the street, garments flapping, with the dogs jumping around her once more, barking at her heels.

Katya hurried on and was glad to turn in at her own gate. She would need to get some supper out quickly. Everyone must be starving by now. She opened the front door, welcoming the warmth of the house after the bitter cold outside. She was bent over pulling off her boots when Peter came into the front room. She smiled at him and started to tell him about MaryAnn when he interrupted her.

"It's on the radio. The Japanese have bombed Pearl Harbor."

Part 3:
Wartime

The War Declaration and Christmas, 1941

"Good evening, Mr. and Mrs. America and all the ships at sea."

Katya and Peter sat in the front room listening intently to Walter Winchell on the radio. Winchell's staccato delivery punctuated by the sounds of a telegraph in the background gave urgency to his report. "Flash! Today, December eighth, nineteen forty-one, the United States Congress, with one dissenting vote, passed a declaration of war against Japan. Congresswoman Janet Rankin, Republican, of Montana, was the lone dissenter."

"Edith Fleming was right," Katya told Peter with a heavy heart.

News of the fighting in Europe had already been hard to bear. Katya hadn't heard from her parents in the old country for a long time now. Over the years, she had offered to help them resettle in America, but they always refused. At first, they wrote that they couldn't abandon their home and land, and later, her mother's health deteriorated, and they feared she wouldn't survive the long journey. Since Katya's last few letters hadn't been returned, she clung desperately to the hope her parents were still alive.

During the next weeks, the relentless stream of newspaper headlines burned into Katya's brain: December 10th, *Germany and Italy declare war on U.S.;* December 11th, *Japanese Invade the Philippines;* December 18th, *Russian Troops Besieged by German Forces.*

"Are we going to die, Mama? Because of the war?"

Katya laid down her newspaper and looked into Mari's worried face. "No, Mari. We're not going to die. Many people die in wartime, but our country is far away from the fighting. I hope everything here will be all right."

"What about Johnny and Peter, Jr? Will they have to go and fight?"

"They might, Mari. We'll have to wait and see."

"And Rick?"

"Rick, too. Yes." Katya hugged Mari to her and smoothed her hair, assuring her that, somehow, they would all endure. Then they sat quietly together, the only sound the click, click of the cuckoo clock on the wall above the telephone, its arm jerking back and forth in a stiff rhythm beneath the birdhouse above. Katya had been delighted when her son, Peter Jr., gave her the silly little clock last Christmas, and now its familiar sound served to restore her.

"You could make Johnny a Christmas card," Katya said, "and one for Peter. That would certainly cheer them up."

"I'll make one for Rick, too," Mari said, sliding off the couch and heading out of the room in search of her crayons.

To keep her own sanity, Katya concentrated on preparations for Christmas. She was glad that Christmas at St. Michael's was celebrated on January 7th, the Feast of Three Kings. It gave her one more week. She cleaned and waxed and polished until her arms ached. She scrubbed and bleached and rinsed until her bedding was snow white, and then hung it on the clothesline in the back yard despite the frosty air. When she brought everything in, stiff with cold, the warmth of the kitchen softened the cloth again. Then Katya ironed the sheets and pillowcases and covered first Johnny's bed and then Peter Jr.'s with linens that smelled of sunshine.

A few days before Russian Christmas, Katya stood before a large tub filled with flour, checking off the other baking ingredients on the kitchen table. She set a little pan of water on the stove, water she would heat later and use to activate her yeast. "But there's no yeast!" she muttered, scanning the icebox shelves in irritation. She pulled off her apron and went to gather up her coat and pocketbook. After a quick check of the cupboard for other things she might need, Katya headed out the door and rounded the corner to Churlin's Grocery.

The bell above the door tinkled as Katya stepped inside the store. She saw Steve on the familiar orange crate in front of the window. He sat, arms folded, with his second chin resting on his chest. Steve peered at Katya over his glasses as the back door slammed and his son Willie appeared carrying cartons of soup and evaporated milk. Anna, who had been stacking cans on a shelf, bustled over as the radio chattered softly in the background.

"We just heard," Anna said. "The men will be called up any day now."

Katya could feel fear clutching her stomach.

"Those from eighteen to forty-four can be called for military service."

"Up to forty-four?" Katya said. "Thank God that at least Peter Sr. is too old."

"They won't take him, anyway," Willie said, setting a carton on the counter. "Too many years' experience in the steel mill. Experienced men will be spared because of their jobs."

"They didn't take Willie, either," Anna said.

"I tried to enlist," he explained, "but I was rejected. Bad Ticker."

"Thank God," Katya said.

"Old Four-F Willie," the rotund man scoffed sadly. "Who wants to be Four-F?"

"I'm glad they wouldn't take him," Anna said quietly to Katya, and then louder, she added, "Who'd run the store with you gone? Your father and I couldn't manage alone."

"They won't take your Peter Jr,. either," Willie said, slitting open one of the cartons and placing cans on the counter. "Not with his bad eyes. I saw them reject a guy with bad eyes when I tried to get in. If Peter Jr. ever broke his glasses, he couldn't tell who was the enemy."

"You really think they'd reject him?" Katya desperately wanted to believe him.

"I'm sure of it," Willie answered. "No way they'd take Junior."

Katya's heart was suddenly lighter. She picked out a few more items and then decided on some lunch meat.

"Steve!" Anna called. "A half pound of pickle pimento."

"Sliced on the machine," Katya added, watching Steve rise from his crate and waddle over to the butcher's block. He had a habit of cutting lunch meat by hand into thick, uneven slabs while the new automatic slicer sat unused beside him.

Probably too lazy to clean the machine every time, Katya thought.

Steve took a square loaf out of the refrigerated case, flipped a switch on the machine, and pushed the meat into the whirling blade. Thin slices rolled away into a neat pile. He scooped up the meat with paper and slapped it onto the scale, rising on tiptoe to read the amount. "One-half pound. Twenty-nine cents."

Katya's brow wrinkled as she looked at the meat on the scale and then at the butcher's thumb, which was pressing down on one corner. Katya looked Steve straight in the eye. "One-half pound," she marveled, "Who would have guessed?" She stood her ground and waited. Slowly, Steve slid his thumb off the scale and lurched back to the machine. He returned with four more slices, added them to the scale, and then wrapped the meat and handed it to her. "And six cakes of yeast," she said. Whenever she got angry at the old fox, Katya would remember how Steve and Anna had allowed her a long line of credit during the Depression. She knew they'd helped other people, too.

Back home again, Katya threw herself into the task at hand. Never one to measure, she sifted ingredients into the tub with a narrowed eye, creating her dough. She kneaded it to just the right consistency, let it rise, and then kneaded again. Separating the dough, she braided some of it and then laid long braided loaves onto cookie sheets. Other dough was spread flat, sprinkled with a thick layer of nuts and sugar, then drizzled with melted butter and rolled into a jelly roll. Puffy poppy seed buns dotted other pans. Finally, Katya covered every pan with a fresh dish towel and placed it between the clean sheets on her bed. Gently, she laid a thick feather comforter over everything.

After the dough had time to rise again, Katya slid one loaf after another into the oven, quickly brushing the tops with beaten egg. Before long, the fragrance of baking bread cheered her kitchen, and Katya was piling golden brown loaves onto the counter. She coated her poppy seed rolls with honey and then carried everything to the unheated back porch in readiness for Christmas Eve. Tomorrow, she would begin her pastries.

Katya had been working for days with fierce determination. She couldn't do anything about the war, but if her sons were going to leave her, they would leave on a full stomach. Besides, Willie told her there was no way they would take Peter Jr.

At dusk on January 6th, with the air in the kitchen damp from steaming pots on the stove, Katya heard Mari calling. "We're ready, Mama. Come look!"

As she wiped her hands on her apron and went into the front room, the smell of pine greeted her. She saw Mari and Papa standing in front of the big tree in the corner, its multicolor lights winking through the gathering darkness. They smiled expectantly.

"It's the most beautiful tree we've ever had!" Katya exclaimed.

"You say that every year," Mari answered, but she was obviously pleased by Katya's response.

"No doubt about it, Mari. This tree is the best one yet," Katya praised the lights and the homemade ornaments, especially the small angel Mari made only yesterday. The sound of stamping feet echoed from the porch, and Peter Jr. pushed open the door, bringing a puff of blowing snow inside with him. MaryAnn and Rick were close behind.

"Look who I found wanting to give away presents!" Peter Jr. chortled and pulled off his fogged-up glasses to wipe them with a handkerchief. *Thank God for those glasses,* Katya thought, remembering Willie's words. Soon after, Helen came home from work, and then Bettie, who had taken a part-time job at the dime store for the Christmas season.

The girls hurried in to set the table while Rick and Peter Jr. found extra chairs. Soon, everything was ready.

"I'll light the candles," MaryAnn said. She held a match to the two smaller candles at each end of the table and then to the tall one in the center.

"For the star of Bethlehem," Mari said solemnly, then turned off the kitchen light. The glow of the Christmas tree from the front room merged through the doorway into the candlelight in the kitchen as Katya laid her apron aside.

"Where's Johnny?" Helen asked. "He's late."

"Where else?" Peter Jr. said. "He's still out Christmas shopping. Same as he was last year at this time."

"We'll go ahead without him," Papa said. "The food is hot, and everyone else is here." Chairs scraped as they found places at the table.

"I can't understand why he does this," Bettie complained, looking at the empty chair next to Peter Jr.

Papa bowed his head and waited. When he began to speak, his voice was soft. "Heavenly Father, we ask your blessing on this food and on those gathered here." The prayer was longer than usual that night as Papa prayed for peace. Katya saw MaryAnn move a little closer to Rick, and the faces around the table grew somber. She found herself hoping the empty chair across from her wasn't somehow an omen for the future.

"John had better hurry," Rick said later to Katya, "or all this great food will be gone."

"I can't understand why he insists on shopping at the last minute," Bettie pouted.

"Because he's a tightwad," Peter Jr. laughed. "He's the ultimate bargain hunter, snapping up the last-minute markdowns."

"Well, you should make him stop, Mama," Bettie went on. "He has no consideration for you or for the rest of us."

"He does, too! He picked mushrooms for Mama's soup, didn't he?" Mari said defensively. "He even let me hold the pillowcase."

"Pillowcase?" Helen asked.

"It's what we put the mushrooms in," Mari explained. "When we're out in the woods, Johnny gathers mushrooms, and then I open the pillowcase so he can drop them in." Katya had to smile. No one could ever get away with criticizing Johnny if Mari was around.

"I hope he can tell the mushrooms from the toadstools," Rick said.

"Yep," Peter Jr. chimed in. "I'd hate to see Bettie keel over, it being Christmas and all."

"Sticks and stones," Bettie replied haughtily and helped herself to more soup.

Finally, halfway through the meal, Johnny showed up. He apologized and then slid into the chair next to Peter Jr.

"El cheapo lives!" Junior said.

"You can thank me after dinner," Johnny answered him, grinning, "when you open your splendid gift."

"Just so it's better than last year," Peter Jr. replied. "Talk about a cheesy present."

"What do you mean cheesy?" Johnny asked, stung. "That was a great guitar!"

"Says who?"

"Says the guy at the shop."

"The pawn shop," Junior corrected him. "You bought me a guitar from a pawn shop."

"So what? The guy told me it was a great guitar. He called it a quality instrument."

"Some quality! He wouldn't even take it back."

Johnny looked pained, "You took it back?"

"I said I tried. He wouldn't take it."

"I can't believe you took back my guitar."

"It wasn't your guitar." Peter Jr. replied. "You gave it to me. And you owe me fifty cents."

"What for?"

"That's what it cost me to get the guy to take it."

Katya joined in the laughter and stood up to put the coffee on.

"You register for the draft yet?" Rick asked Johnny. The room grew quiet.

"Yep. But I'll wait to be called up. You?"

"I thought of going down and just signing up, you know. They'll get all of us anyway," Rick said. "But MaryAnn thought I should wait."

"She's right, Rick. They'll take single guys first. No sense rushing things."

"Willie Churlin says they won't take Peter Jr. because of his eyes," Katya said.

"God, I hope so," Johnny turned to Peter Jr. "Maybe one of us could stay out."

"It's too late." Peter Jr. said. "I signed up yesterday."

Katya's legs felt rubbery as the floor seemed to shift under her. She sat back down again, looking at Peter Jr. in disbelief.

"I was going to tell you, Mom," he said uncomfortably. "I just wanted to
wait until everyone else was here. I enlisted in the Air Corps."

"But your eyes," Katya said. "What about your eyes?"

"I memorized the chart. The line was so long I had plenty of time. By the time I got up to the front, I could have recited the letters backward, too."

"Whew!" Johnny said as Katya sat, stunned.

"I want to do my part. I couldn't watch everyone else go off and leave me behind. Besides, this way, I pick the service. I don't want to go into the infantry."

Nobody said anything. Then Johnny started thumping him on the back. "My little brother," he said gruffly, then brushed a hand across his eyes.

Rick pushed his chair back and stood up with a broad grin, coming over to pump Junior's hand. Papa stood and went over to Peter Jr., as well. As he stood there hugging his son, Katya could sense the pride mingled with the tears in his father's eyes.

"Those Germans better watch out, "Rick chortled, "now that Peter Jr. is on his way."

"Does this mean all the men will be gone?" Helen asked, picking at her food morosely. "What kind of life is that?"

Mari, caught up in the sudden excitement, was dancing up and down. Peter Jr. pulled her up on his lap, and she hugged him as he jiggled her up and down on one knee. Katya looked at them and willed her mouth into an encouraging smile.

"Can girls join?" Bettie interrupted. "I'm going to join, too."

"Don't be silly, monkey face. They just want guys."

"Bettie, don't talk like that. Why would you even think of such a thing!" Katya's voice was louder than she meant, but suddenly, it was all too much. Her parents were lost somewhere in the madness in Europe. The girl didn't know what she was saying, and now ominous forces were snatching away her son. She shivered.

Later, everyone went to Midnight Mass and then went home to open presents. Before shooing Mari off to bed, Katya produced another sumptuous buffet. She laid out cold ham along with her *hrudka,* homemade egg cheese, and thick slices of different breads with butter. There was Steve Churlin's homemade sausage, cold beets laced with horseradish, and a tangy bean salad. The pastries produced the usual *ahhs* of appreciation. As she watched Peter Jr. heaping his plate high, Katya felt a sudden lump in her throat.

"You must be exhausted, Mama," MaryAnn said, coming up beside her. "Sit down, and I'll fix you a plate."

"Not just yet," Katya replied as the dread she had been holding at bay for so long threatened to engulf her. "I'm really not very hungry."

Peter Goes to Boot Camp

On the day Peter Jr. left for basic training, Mari went downtown to the bus station with Mama and Papa to see him off. Because they were early, Peter Jr. said he wouldn't mind a Coca-Cola at Abram's Drug Store on the way. A last look at the old neighborhood, he called it.

Mr. Abram came over to serve them himself. Hearing Peter Jr. was going to boot camp, he shook his hand before they left and said the Cokes were on the house.

A big crowd was gathered at the bus station by the time they got there, with people milling around alongside empty buses lined up in the parking lot. The American flag hanging above the doorway fluttered in the breeze, and some people were carrying little flags. Mari nudged Mama, pointing out a young couple pasted up against each other in an embrace.

"Air Corps in front of this bus!" a tall, spare man in a blue uniform called.

He stood straight as a ruler with a clipboard in his hand.

There was a flurry of hugging, and Mama fumbled in her purse and brought out her camera. "Stand next to your brother, Mari. Hurry!"

Peter Jr. took Mari's hand, and they squinted together into the sunlight. Then, Mari took a picture of Peter Jr. with her parents.

"Make sure you don't cut off our heads," Peter Jr. laughed.

"Airmen line up over here!"

Peter Jr. kissed each of them and picked up his duffel bag, hurrying into line. He fell in at the end, taller than most, lanky, with his jacket hanging loosely on his frame.

"Answer 'here' when I call your name." The man looked down at his list. "Anderson."

"Here!" Mari turned to see the boy with the girl still attached to him trying to get away. There was a ripple of laughter, but the voice barked again and cut it off.

"Get in line, Anderson! There's a war going on!"

When all the names were called and it was time to board the bus, musicians broke into the Air Corps song. People all around started waving their flags. Peter Jr. turned and smiled when it was his turn to step inside the bus, and Mari grinned back, excited but uneasy at the same time. She could see Papa blinking back tears.

"He's so thin," Mama said, dabbing her eyes. "I knew I should have made him take sandwiches."

They stood waving goodbye until the bus disappeared around the corner. Mari's stomach seemed to have a big empty space as soon as the bus was out of sight. No one said much on the way home or for the rest of the day, either.

A few weeks later, Mari sat alone at the kitchen table, chin in hand. All the while she took up space in the house alongside Mama and the rest of the family, there was another whole life that she lived only in her head. So while her body walked and talked and ate and got up and went to school, it was in her head that she tried to figure things out, like what to think about the war, and would she ever have a pure heart the way Father Papp said children should, and how to get Ronald Goldenstern to like her.

With Peter Jr. away in the Air Corps, the house was strangely quiet. On Saturday, Mari walked alone to the drug store to buy an ice cream cone. Before this, Mama always made Peter Jr. take her to Abrams, and on the way home he always managed to eat a big part of her ice cream himself. Mari had always gotten mad when he said he'd lick the cone down so it wouldn't drip. She would imagine herself all grown up and buying her own ice cream. She even pictured Peter Jr. on his knees, begging for just one taste. Mari thought about how she would brush a careless finger across the top and let him have only the tiniest lick from her fingertip. But now, walking home without him, Mari was surprised to find that she missed him. Eating all the ice cream herself wasn't nearly as much fun as she thought it would be.

Earlier that afternoon, they'd read Peter Jr.'s letter from camp. He said he was training to be a clerk. His poor eyesight made him ineligible for combat. Mari could see the relief in Mama's face, and she hummed a little tune and zipped around the house afterward, tidying things up.

On Friday, Mama said she'd start a novena, hoping that Johnny and Rick might somehow be spared, as well.

A few days later, Mama sent Mari to Churlin's grocery store for a bag of flour. She heard Willie talking to one of the customers. "The Germans could be bombing us any day now. They'll target those steel mills first thing, you mark my words."

But when Mrs. Churlin gave a little nod in Mari's direction, Willie looked at her and stopped short. He turned away and got busy stocking the shelves. Mari tucked the flour under her arm and ran home.

"Mama, Willie says the Germans will bomb the mills! Is it true?"

Mama looked up from the ironing board, where she was finishing up one of Papa's shirts.

"Will the bombs fall on our house, Mama? Are we going to die?" Mari could feel the fear in her stomach. She watched Mama put her iron down.

"We don't know if the Germans will send planes here, Mari. Probably not. We're a long way from where the fighting is." But she must have seen the look in Mari's eyes. "Don't worry. Worry won't help, anyway. Pray. I'm sure Almighty God will protect us. "

Mari had always believed Mama was right about everything. Now, for the first time, she wasn't sure. So many things had been changing lately. What if Mama was wrong about the bombs? What if Almighty God wasn't listening? Mari already knew Papa could be wrong. But then, she had suspected it all along. It happened on a breezy Saturday afternoon. Mama was shooing her out the door to confession. Mari's first communion, not all that long ago, was still fresh in her mind.

Confession

"Hurry. You'll be late," Mama fussed as Mari struggled into her jacket and zipped it up. "Confession is important, so think carefully about your sins. You talked back to me just last night, remember?"

Mari sighed. Her sin load always grew heavier with Mama on the job.

"What about prayer? Did you remember your prayers every day?"

With the question ringing in her ears, Mari fled out the door, down the porch steps, and into the street. She always felt a lump in her throat before confession, awed at being pulled up in front of Almighty God. And telling the secrets hidden in her heart right out loud in front of Father Papp was no picnic, either. She supposed she'd get the hang of it someday, but for now, it was scary stuff. Mari sighed and wondered if she could ever hope to be pure of heart.

Later, as she knelt behind the altar ticking off the commandments in her head, she recited all the sins she could remember. She finished with, "And I cut on Sunday."

"What?" She felt Father Papp turn toward her in spite of himself. He had never looked at her in confession before. She felt herself stammering.

"Cut ... with scissors. I cut out paper dolls on Sunday."

"That's not a sin." Mari couldn't be sure, but a little smile seemed to be playing around the corner of Father's mouth.

"Mama said it wasn't, either!" Mari blurted. "But Papa said it was!" She remembered Papa's scowl when he told her that Sunday was not a time for worldly pleasures. Sunday, he said, was God's day—a day of rest. That's why the stores were closed and people stayed at home with their families.

Since Mari loved cutting out her dolls, she had sided with Mama in the argument. But there in church, with the Eye of God painted above the altar looking straight at her, Mari decided she'd better confess anyway, just in case.

"Tell your Papa Sunday recreation is not a sin. That idea died with the Puritans. Now, make a good act of contrition."

Papa didn't say anything when Mari told him what Father had said. But that wasn't new. Often, when she tried talking to him, Papa seemed to answer from some great distance. Mari could never figure out how to lure him any closer to her or find a way to get over to where he was.

The next day, Lillian came over in the afternoon, and they played movie stars. Lillian was Joan Crawford, and Mari was Betty Grable. After they picked out their husbands (Mari always picked Dennis Morgan), Lillian brought out the table and chairs Mari got last Christmas and set them under the big tree in the side yard. Mari fetched pocketbooks with Mama's old beads in them, high heels Helen didn't wear anymore, and cast-off Sunday hats with torn veils. Then, since they didn't really know what movie stars did all day long, they played house.

Afterward, eating homemade bread and butter at the kitchen table, Mari told Lillian about Ronald Goldenstern. "I like him," Mari blushed, "but he doesn't notice me."

"Call him up."

Lillian's words hit her like a shot. Call up Ronald? Weren't boys supposed to call girls? Boys were always calling Helen—at least they did before the war. But then Helen never had trouble getting boys to notice her.

"Ronald can't notice you if you don't talk to him," Lillian said, helping herself to another slice of bread. She spread it thick with butter, and, chewing slowly, she walked out the door.

Call up Ronald? Mari shivered. *What if he gets mad? What if he hangs up on me?* She pictured Ronald's face in front of her. She saw his hair falling in black and shiny waves onto his forehead. She remembered his smooth skin and dark eyes fringed with thick lashes when he looked down at his desk. Mari's face felt warm, and she hugged her arms to her chest. She made up her mind. With Mama out of the house, if she was ever going to act, it was now. With fingers tingling, she rushed to look up his number and dial before she could change her mind.

"Hello." It was a woman's voice. Mari had been sure Ronald would answer.

"Is … is Ronald there?"

"No. Who is this?"

Mari's heart lurched at the stern tone on the other end. She felt faint. "It's I'm … it's … one of his classmates."

"He's not here. I don't know when he'll be back."

"Oh. Well … I'm sorry to bother you. Thank you very much."

Mari's face was on fire as she hung up the phone. That had to be Ronald's mother. She sounded cultured. She sounded cold. The next day at school, Ronald came charging up to Mari in front of everyone.

"Did you call me up?" he demanded angrily.

"How did you know it was me?" she asked, taken by surprise.

"I'm one of his classmates," Ronald mimicked in a singsong voice. "My mother said the girl who called had a good vocabulary and was very polite." But the way Ronald said it made it sound like a slap.

"I wouldn't call him again for all the money in the world!" she told MaryAnn later as they sat in her bedroom. She said how Ronald embarrassed her in front of all the kids.

"Well, you do have some vocabulary," MaryAnn said kindly. "But that's good. It's an indication you're smart."

"Fat lot of good that is!" Mari shrugged, thinking she should have paid attention when Helen said boys never liked smart girls. Helen had never minded having trouble back when she was in high school. She said there were plenty of boys eager to help her with her homework.

"I wouldn't worry about Ronald," MaryAnn went on. "Lots of boys will pay attention to you later on. You'll see."

"Well, at least I'm short," Mari sighed. "Helen says tall boys always like short girls best."

Mari made it a point to ignore Ronald from then on. She even tossed her hair and turned up her nose as she walked by but, sneaking a look back, she could see he never paid attention to her.

Mrs. Sturgill and Bettie

Mr. Sturgill, Papa's boss at the steel plant, asked him if one of his daughters might be able to help Mrs. Sturgill with her housework. She, being a diabetic, was extremely frail and had just lost her housekeeper of many years. So Mama sent MaryAnn to work one day a week at the Sturgills. And now that Bettie was fifteen, Mama sent her along one day to see whether she might take her sister's place.

"Imagine living in such a grand house," Bettie breathed excitedly as she followed MaryAnn up the path to the impressive brick house on the hill.

"You're not going to live here, Bettie. You've come to work. And watch your step. Mrs Sturgill is very particular, and she can be mean."

But Bettie scarcely heard, so great was her eagerness to meet the woman who lived in such a palace.

But nothing MaryAnn could have said would have prepared Bettie for the woman who opened the door that morning. Hermoine Sturgill was pencil thin, close to emaciated, with skin stretched so tightly over her cheekbones that it radiated a porcelain gloss. Her hair, hennaed to a bright orange, frizzed in a militant halo around her skull. Her hands were large, with bony fingers ending in manicured nails polished to a hard red sheen.

But it was her outfit, an oriental ensemble with a jade-green jacket above pajama-like trousers etched in an intricate pattern, that took Bettie by surprise. Bettie had never seen such clothes.

"You're late."

Bettie could see the color begin to rise in MaryAnn's cheeks. But before she could manage a reply, Mrs. Sturgill had already turned her attention to Bettie.

"And who might you be?"

"I'm Bettie, MaryAnn's sister. And I've come to help," she said, stepping forward and looking the woman straight in the eye.

"I've only hired one girl. I won't pay for two."

"I don't ask for pay. I've come to learn. Then, if I'm suitable, I can take over for MaryAnn. She's old enough for a full-time job uptown."

And that was how Bettie came to work for Mrs. Sturgill. And where MaryAnn had been cowed by her employer, Bettie looked on her with endless fascination. She loved seeing her exotic wardrobe and working among so many fine things. She would pretend she was the lady of the house and that the fine china and ornate silver were her own.

Later, when MaryAnn got a full-time job at Sears, Bettie did take her place. Over time, Mrs. Sturgill seemed to dote on Bettie and even began giving her some castoff garments.

"She never gave me anything," MaryAnn said, running her fingers over the soft cashmere sweater Bettie had brought home.

"Mrs. Sturgill likes me," Bettie said proudly. "She likes me a lot."

At summer's end, when it was time for Bettie to go back to school, Mrs. Sturgill said it would be better for Bettie to transfer to Horace Mann High instead of remaining at her inner-city school. Graduating from Mann, she said, would assure Bettie of a good job when she graduated and a better start in life. All she needed to do was to give the Sturgill address as her own, and she would tell the school officials that Bettie was a relative staying with them during the school term.

Elated, Bettie told Mama about Mrs. Sturgill's plan.

"How does it help you get a better start in life when you begin with a lie?" Mama demanded.

But her veto only made Bettie's determination greater, and she told Mrs. Sturgill about Mama's reaction. A few nights later, she overheard Mama and Papa talking in the kitchen. Mr. Sturgill had called Papa into his office after work. He talked about how parents were obliged to do everything they could to help their children succeed. Mrs. Sturgill felt Bettie should go to Horace Mann and was even willing to ease the way for her. A better school could offer Bettie opportunities that her present school could not. Surely, they would not want to stand in their daughter's way. Papa eventually persuaded Mama that

Bettie deserved her chance. Bettie transferred to Mann and was soon elbow-to-elbow with the city's upper crust.

"Who's the new girl?" Bettie overheard a tall blonde whisper as she walked down the hall at her new school.

"Bettie Cmar. She lives with the Sturgills, her aunt and uncle, over on Chestnut," said her short friend, who turned away when Bettie smiled uncertainly in her direction.

"Well, she must be their ward or something," the blonde continued. "She doesn't belong here."

Bettie shrank inwardly, hating her faded sweater and limp skirt, passed first from Helen down to MaryAnn and now to her. Except for Mrs. Sturgill's castoffs, she did look out of place. When some of the girls tried to question her about her life, she made vague comments and changed the subject. Because she said little and stayed to herself so much, the others eventually lost interest and left her alone, as well.

Horace Mann prided itself on having the city's highest percentage of students who took the college preparatory course. The program was overwhelmingly male except for the few girls who hoped to go on to teachers' college. Aspiring nurses took the general education course and would get their training after graduation at the city hospital.

"For you, I recommend the Commercial Program," the guidance counselor advised, inclining her marcelled head in Bettie's direction. "Mann's graduates can expect interviews with the leading companies in Gary," she added smugly. "Typing skills are paramount."

After school, MaryAnn could hardly wait to hear Bettie's news. "What's it like? Are the kids nice? Are they stuck up?" MaryAnn wanted to know as they stood drying the dishes in the kitchen.

"The kids are all right," Bettie said curtly.

"How about the boys? Are the boys dreamy?"

"Some," Bettie shrugged. "But it doesn't matter. The commercial classes are all girls, anyway." Bettie realized from the first day that even if she made friends, she couldn't invite them home. And how could she date when the boy might tell school authorities where she really lived? But she didn't say any of this to MaryAnn, who had sided with Mama and against her going to Mann in the first place.

While each male student at Mann was required to take at least one semester of woodshop, girls took a semester of sewing and another of cooking. Having taken cooking at her old school, Bettie enrolled in Clothing One. Gifted with imagination and having seen fine clothes at her job with the Sturgills, Bettie began to create. While she couldn't buy expensive cloth, she had a good eye and used color, instead. The other girls bought designer patterns, but Bettie took the cheapest, simplest patterns and added her own innovations. The sewing teacher took notice and started encouraging Bettie to explore her talent. Before long, she took another clothing class as an elective, and her wardrobe improved.

"Pretty jumper, Bettie. Is it new?" the tall blonde wanted to know, coming up to her in the cafeteria.

Her short companion joined them and smiled. "I noticed the blouse with the cap sleeves you had on yesterday with the gored skirt. Very stylish. That's new as well, isn't it?"

"I'm Veronica," the blonde said, slipping her arm through Bettie's. "You could sit with us at lunch today. We have room at our table."

So Bettie sat with the girls and their small clique in the cafeteria that day and the next, but she shunned their advances when they tried to learn more about her.

When Mrs. Sturgill asked her about school one day, Bettie told her about what the sewing teacher said about her having a real talent for design. Mrs. Sturgill was enthusiastic and praised her warmly. Bettie reveled in her approval. They began to have little talks in the kitchen when she was finished with her work.

"She thinks I'm special, Mama. I can tell she really likes me," Bettie said proudly. She started to grow dissatisfied with things at home: the old-fashioned way Mama dressed, the way their dishes and silverware didn't match, and the worn spots on the davenport in the front room.

A yearly highlight at Mann was the Spring Fashion Show, put on by the home economics department. The girls would model outfits they had worked on throughout the year. This year's class was bigger than usual, and Miss Harris, the sewing teacher, expected the show to be the best ever.

When the big night arrived, Bettie stood backstage watching the other girls peeking through the curtains to spot their families in the audience. Mama wouldn't be here, of course, or MaryAnn. *But Mari's here.* She smiled at her skinny little seven-year-old sister clinging to her backstage. Mari would be one of the models, Bettie having made them "Big Sister, Little Sister" outfits. Such matching ensembles hadn't been worn in past years.

The teacher had been enthusiastic when Bettie mused about the possibility one day in class. She hadn't realized, she said, that Bettie even had a little sister. Horrified, Bettie made excuses, but when Miss Harris latched onto an idea, there was no arguing with her. Bettie agreed, believing she had no other choice.

Before they left home that night, Bettie told Mari what to expect if she blabbed about their family or where they lived. "One word, and you die," she warned.

But she needn't have worried, seeing how terrified Mari looked grasping the hand of the freshman girl who would look after her backstage until it was her time to go out.

"Our next model is Bettie Cmar," Miss Harris announced. "She is wearing a smart navy street dress trimmed with white piping around the collar and the pockets." Bettie paraded down the runway and then hurried offstage to change.

Later on in the program, Bettie stepped onto the runway ahead of Mari "in their matching spring coats in a soft peach color. Notice," Miss Harris was saying, "that both coats are fully lined." As Bettie opened her coat to reveal the patterned lining, she hoped Mari would remember to do the same. "Underneath, they are wearing sheaths belted at the waist in the same patterned fabric."

"Both girls love wearing hats. Bettie's is her own creation, a brimless beehive with a radiant spray of pastel flowers and a short illusion veil."

Moving down the runway, Bettie's smile felt chiseled onto her face. As she paused at the end, waiting for Mari, she swallowed hard, feeling faint. Then, from some great distance, she seemed to hear applause. Turning, she saw Mari bouncing toward her. "This is Mari, ladies and gentlemen. Isn't she adorable," Miss Harris purred, "in her own peach ensemble with its matching tam o' shanter? She wears it at a rakish angle atop her long brown hair."

Mari turned and added a spontaneous little curtsey before going to stand beside Bettie. When Mari grinned up at her, Bettie could feel her face relax, and they walked back hand-in-hand to approving murmurs from the audience.

The highlight of the show was the evening gown presentation. One after another, girls paraded down the runway in soft satin gowns, two with a daring slit up the side. But Bettie, the final model, appeared center stage, frozen in the spotlight wearing a voluminous cotton skirt with red peppermint stripes dancing diagonally across a dazzling white background. "The off-the-shoulder bodice features frothy puffed sleeves billowing out on either side," Miss Harris trilled. "Frivolous accents that highlight her tiny waist."

The effect, a complete break from the fashion of the day, was stunning.

Later, flanked by the other models, Bettie stood center stage in the final tableau of the evening.

Miss Harris, flushed with pleasure, acknowledged the generous applause. "Thank you for your attendance," she told the audience. "It should be noted that both Junior and Senior girls will be wearing these lovely formals to the Junior/Senior Prom."

Why does she have to ruin a perfect evening? Bettie thought. Dateless, she would go back home, hang her formal in the closet, and content herself with having achieved her goal. She had survived a year at Mann. A good job was surely in her future. Never again would she be hiding out, the one who didn't fit, the girl from the wrong side of the tracks.

"Congratulations, Bettie. You looked swell up there."

Bettie looked up into the handsome face of Royce Van Allen. She had seen him in the hallway over the year but couldn't remember ever standing this close. She saw that his eyes beneath the shock of blonde hair that spilled onto his forehead were a startling blue. She could feel the warmth creeping up her neck.

"Thank you." Her tongue felt thick in her mouth.

"I didn't want to come tonight. Not a guy thing, you know." He gave a little shrug, and when he laughed, Bettie felt a delicious tickle travel the full length of her spine. "But since my sister was in the show, mother wouldn't let me off the hook."

Bettie nodded, thinking of the thick-waisted Clare Van Allen and marveling that fraternal twins could look so different.

"You looked like a confection up there, Bettie. I wondered, spur of the moment, whether you had a date for the prom."

"Why, no," she blurted.

"Good. Then you'll go with me."

Bettie wanted to bite off her tongue right then and there, but her flustered manner only seemed to amuse the supremely confident boy in front of her.

"We have to go home, Bettie. Mama says I can't stay up too late." Bettie felt Mari beside her, tugging at her dress

"Hello, princess! So you're Bettie's sister! You looked pretty cute on stage tonight."

Bettie saw Mari's face light up with pleasure, and she quickly snatched up the small hand and gripped it hard, fearing such compliments could make Mari forget to keep her mouth shut. She made some excuse about forgetting to gather up the rest of her clothes and hurried into the girls' bathroom. They waited a very long time before coming back out. Bettie breathed a sigh of relief when she saw Royce was gone.

Later that night, she pulled MaryAnn into the bedroom and told her what had happened.

"Royce Van Allen?" MaryAnn planted herself on the bed and tucked one leg under her. "Isn't he the one you told me about?"

"Plays baseball. President of the debating club. His parents are some kind of society people. Royce plans to go to college, of course." Just saying his name brought the tickle down Bettie's spine again. "Royce Van Allen wants to take me to the prom!" She was looking at MaryAnn with a mixture of delight and agony.

"So what are you going to do?"

"I don't know!" she wailed. "Isn't there some way I could manage to go?"

"You could ask Mama," MaryAnn said uncertainly. "Maybe she could
come up with an idea."

"Mama?" Bettie's face fell. "Pooh! You always want to ask Mama everything. Last time I tried to talk to her about going to the prom, she said I could take Johnny!"

"She was only trying to figure out a way for you to go, Bettie. And to make sure you keep your secret so that you'll graduate. Besides," she added weakly, "I'll bet some girls have gone to the prom with their brothers."

"Would you?" The look on MaryAnn's face confirmed the answer she'd known all along.

The following week, Royce stopped to talk to Bettie in the hallway between classes. She would find him waiting for her when she came out of the typing room, and she basked in the envy reflected in the other girls' eyes. But inside, her stomach was churning. The prom was not far off, and she knew she would have to do something. That Saturday, Bettie found Mrs. Sturgill smoking a late-afternoon cigarette in the kitchen. With the smoke curling between them, she tried to explain her dilemma. After she finished, Mrs. Sturgill leaned back in her chair and regarded Bettie with a critical eye. "So, what is it you want from me, Bettie?"

"I'm not exactly sure," she confessed. "I just wondered whether … hoped, really … that there was some way I might go with Royce to the prom," she finished, her voice trailing off.

Mrs. Sturgill frowned and leaned back in her chair. "And how might you accomplish that?"

Last night, Bettie had imagined Mrs. Sturgill allowing her to dress at the grand house and Royce taking her to the dance from there. But now, watching those bony fingers tap, tapping her cigarette into the tiny ashtray and Mrs. Sturgill merely blowing another long stream of smoke through her nostrils, Bettie just wanted to go home.

"Well, I'm sure you'll let me know how things turn out," she said as Bettie gathered up her things and rushed from the kitchen. Halfway down the walk, she realized she had left her sweater and turned back to the house. She went to tell Mrs. Sturgill she'd returned when she heard a voice in the library.

"Leticia? Hermoine Sturgill. My dear, I simply had to call you. I'm afraid I have a confession to make."

Bettie listened, mortified, as Mrs. Sturgill laid out her story.

"I was simply trying to help the girl, and she fairly jumped at the chance to better herself. The parents? Foreigners. The father works for Reg out at the plant. Well," she sighed, "I was certain you'd want Royce to know."

Monday morning, Royce was waiting for Bettie as she showed up for school.

"Say, Bettie, I've been meaning to talk to you."

"What is it?"

"Something's come up. I … well, I've had this long-standing commitment to Faunile Gray for, well, for a long time. So, I thought it would be best to cancel our prom date. Faunile and I, we've had this understanding for a very long time. And I wouldn't feel right leaving her in the lurch on prom night. You understand, don't you?"

Bettie heard a rushing sound in her ears, and, nodding blindly, she turned and fled down the hall.

MaryAnn Goes to Colorado

"Where's Mama? I have to talk to her." MaryAnn's voice was urgent, but when she saw the look on Bettie's face, she stopped.

"What's wrong, Bettie? You look terrible."

Bettie pulled MaryAnn into the house. In the bedroom, she poured out the whole story.

"Well, good riddance! Lucky you don't have to go to the dance with a creep like that!"

And when Bettie fell sobbing into her arms, MaryAnn stroked her hair and told her everything would be all right.

"Why do you want to talk to Mama?" Bettie asked later when MaryAnn handed her a handkerchief, and she sat wiping her eyes.

"Rick has orders to ship out. He wants me to come to the Army base camp in Colorado."

"Ship out?" Suddenly, the reality of the war fell like a giant dead weight into the room. MaryAnn sat huddled in a timid heap on the corner of the bed. "Can't Rick come home first?"

"He said if I'd go there, we could be together a few days longer."

"Don't you want to go?"

"No. Yes. Well, I mean, of course, I do."

"So, what's the matter?"

"Oh, Bettie, I'm afraid! I'm afraid about Rick's going away. I'm afraid he might be hurt—killed even—and I'm scared of going all that way alone. I've never traveled anywhere by myself."

Bettie wished she were the one going on a trip. Not to Rick, of course. She couldn't understand why MaryAnn had married him in the first place. She should have held out for someone with a future. But Rick had been so persistent, he'd finally worn her down.

"I came to ask if Mama thought I should go."

"Of course you should!" Bettie jumped up from the bed and pulled MaryAnn up with her. "Stop being such a ninny! Get on the first bus you can and go to Colorado. You're a married lady, after all!"

"Of course, you'll go," Mama scolded when MaryAnn explained the situation to her. "You have to go to your husband."

Bettie smiled in spite of herself. It was a rare occasion that she and Mama agreed on anything. But Bettie would remember hurrying away so she wouldn't have to listen as MaryAnn told Katya about Mrs. Sturgill's betrayal, her humiliation fresh in her mind.

The next afternoon, MaryAnn bought a Greyhound bus ticket for Colorado, and Mama sent a note to Mrs. Sturgill stating that she should find someone else to work for her on Saturdays. Bettie, she wrote to her, wouldn't be going back there anymore.

After Bettie left, MaryAnn thought back to how her relationship with Rick had started. There was a time in MaryAnn's life, back before the war, when Rick was merely a convenience, someone to pick her up after work or take her to the movies on Saturday night. No one in the family had thought much about him. In those days, as usual, Bettie had been the one to talk about him in a way that made him seem unimportant.

"Rick's awfully quiet," Bettie had said to MaryAnn one night when she'd returned home from a date. "Isn't it dull being with him on a date? What do you talk about? But maybe talking isn't what you like to do when you're alone."

"Of course, we talk," she'd retorted. "Rick's shy until he gets to know people, that's all. And he's just someone to go around with, nothing more."

"I can't believe Rick doesn't dance!" Helen had whispered on a double date at the Danceland. "He just sits there mooning over you and looking miserable." Then she'd made it a point to steer MaryAnn to her friends.

"The dark-haired one over there is Joey's pal, MaryAnn. He's dying to meet you. He's a good dancer and a snappy dresser. Come on, I'll introduce you."

And so, MaryAnn met the dark-haired one. And then a blonde fellow, and another one after that. And later, when they asked her out, she went.

Meanwhile, every night after work, Rick would be waiting at the curb in front of Sears, ready to drive her home. Sometimes, she'd find a single rose wrapped in tissue paper lying on her seat. Most evenings, he would call the house about nine-thirty just to say goodnight, and on Sundays to ask if she cared to go for a drive.

"His car's so old," Helen sniffed. "He slaves in his parents' tavern, and you know his family doesn't have much money. And he should dress up more. Why don't you just tell him to leave you alone?"

Why, indeed? Because MaryAnn was haunted by the pain in Rick's eyes when she told him she was seeing someone else. When she said she'd take the bus for a while, he would be there anyway, waiting. "In case you changed your mind," he'd say in that solemn way of his. If he had only gotten angry or argued with her, it might have been different.

Rick didn't pressure her to "go all the way" like some of the others did. She could let her guard down, feel comfortable and safe with him. As time went on and he'd kissed her with a growing passion, she came to recognize her power over him. She liked it.

"It's not as if I'm going to get married or anything," she'd protested to Helen.

"Why? Has he asked you?"

"Of course. He asks over and over, but it doesn't mean anything. I'm not going to get married for a long, long time."

But now she was on her way to him at his Army base in Colorado. Katya knew that MaryAnn felt a deep longing to be near her husband.

Things don't always work out the way we planned, do they? MaryAnn thought, gazing out the bus window at acre after acre of barren land. Before this trip, she couldn't have imagined the sheer size of the country that she'd lived in all her life. But then, with all that had happened over the past year, she knew there were plenty of other things that she hadn't imagined, either.

Like that hot summer night when everything changed. Rick had dropped over to return the book she'd left in his car, and they were all laughing and talking in the front room, four of them—MaryAnn, Rick, Mama, and Mari. Mama was fanning herself with one of those paper fans she'd brought home from church, the ones Petrin's Funeral Home left in the pews for advertising. They heard the back screen door slam and Papa's voice in the kitchen. Mama got up and hurried out of the room.

MaryAnn remembered how she'd kept on talking, raising her voice, trying to cover up the argument she knew was going on out there. She could hear Papa's voice growing louder. He'd been drinking again, and Mama's softer voice shushing. Suddenly, Papa smashed his way into the room, and when she tried to stop him, he stumbled, knocking her hard against the door jam.

In an instant, Rick was on his feet between them. Papa raised his fist, and just as Rick put up an arm to ward off the blow, Papa lost his balance and fell down hard. Even now, she winced, remembering him lying there, Mari's stricken face, and Mama flustered, trying to smooth things over the way she always did. Then there was Rick's voice, dead quiet, telling Papa to stop it. Stop hurting his family.

Later that night when Rick told her again that he loved her, MaryAnn knew she would marry him. She'd do anything to get out of that house. Almost ten months later, MaryAnn knew she'd made the right decision. She'd made the best decision she would ever make in her life.

"I love being married to you," she'd written in her last letter. "I love eating dinner by candlelight, just the two of us. I love the fun of fixing up a home together and planting our own garden. So it's just a few tomato plants and some carrots, but it's still our garden, isn't it? And I love when we talk about having children. Of course, we'll have children."

"Damn shame. They said World War I was the war to end all wars. Whatever happened to that?" She was listening to the old man several rows in front of her.

84

"Those big shots need cannon fodder, that's all. Glad I did my stint in nineteen seventeen and lived to tell about it. My brother wasn't so lucky."

MaryAnn felt a rush of adrenaline. The next two weeks might be the only future she and Rick would ever have together. Couldn't someone stop those shadowy men bending over maps in a war room somewhere, plotting to send Rick to some godforsaken place to die? *I need him. Need his strength and his gentleness, his kindness and his honesty,* she thought. *Wasn't there some way around this war? Shouldn't someone, somewhere, be able to stop the insanity?*

Stupid question. MaryAnn turned her attention to the slap of the bus wheels on the pavement. That slowed the beat of her heart. The panic was familiar now. It started when Rick wrote they'd be getting their orders right after basic training. Well, of course, he'd be getting orders! Why else had he gone to camp in the first place? The bus was slowing down and MaryAnn could see the town ahead.

"Camp Carson!" the driver called. "Anybody headed for the military base, this is as far as you go."

She looked around and began to gather up her things. No sense in moaning about dangers she hadn't faced yet. Whatever time she and Rick had together would have to last. And it would be glorious! She would see to it. MaryAnn tucked her purse under her arm and headed for the door.

She spotted him right away, standing with his shoulders hunched against the wind. He looked different—taller, leaner, with a leonine quality she'd never caught before. She hesitated, but he was having none of it. He scooped her away even before she reached the last step and kissed her hard right there in front of everyone. She held him tight, soaking up the rough, clean smell of him.

"I got your room," he said with his crooked smile. "We'll go there first." He retrieved her suitcase, and, tucking her hand under his arm, they walked together through the town.

"There are mountains all around us, but you can't see them," he told her. "You'll be able to tomorrow when it's daylight."

"I already saw them from the bus," she said. "My first mountains! How I wished you were there to see them with me."

They were passing a bar, its red and blue sign blinking on and off. "Third Base Tavern, Last Stop Before Home." They could hear the jukebox melody tinkling into the street as a group of servicemen pushed their way outside.

They found the hotel, a small, rustic brown frame building on the main street. She walked ahead of Rick into the reception area.

"'Bout time you showed up!" the woman behind the desk boomed. "This boy was pacin' the lobby here for an hour before you got here, nervous as a polecat. He was afraid you'd changed your mind and gone back home!" MaryAnn couldn't help but warm to the smile that had settled into the woman's leathery face. "Supper's done servin' by eight if you'd care to eat here with us," the woman said, indicating a small dining room. "Your room's up those stairs and to your right."

They barely got the door closed when Rick was pulling her to him. "How long has it been," he muttered, "A year. Maybe two."

"It seems like forever," she breathed, wondering which of them came more eagerly to the embrace. "We have so much to make up for."

He was running his hands over her body, kissing her cheek and her throat, pulling at the buttons on her blouse.

"Wait. Not yet. I've brought something in the suitcase. I want to wear it for you."

Unheeding, he was drawing her sideways onto the bed, and suddenly, what she'd been planning didn't matter. Her face flushed at his touch, and they struggled out of their clothes. As he collapsed onto her, she closed her eyes, and then she was part of him and he was part of her, and she was falling into the wildfire that engulfed them both.

"I thought I wouldn't even get my pants off in time," he chuckled afterward.

"I know. The negligee I'd brought to entice you is still in the suitcase on the floor."

"Who needs a negligee? I like what you're wearing now," He ran his hand down the naked curve of her body. "You were sensational. You must have missed me, too."

She moved closer to him. "I missed you more than I can say. I want us to stay together like this for the rest of our lives."

They barely made it downstairs before the dining room closed. MaryAnn looked around the rustic room with its checkered tablecloths and a chandelier made from antlers hanging in the center. The waitress was a young girl who smiled a lot. She kept asking Rick if he'd like more coffee.

"She likes you," MaryAnn said.

"She likes the uniform," he said. "It makes a difference somehow."

It was true. There was a difference. Not just that Rick was leaner; there was a purpose about him now. As he bent over the menu, she could see they'd clipped his hair so short that his scalp showed through. But his head was beautifully shaped, and his cheekbones in the lamplight looked chiseled from granite.

After dinner, they walked around town. Rick told her she'd be on her own during the days, but he'd come back from camp every evening. On Fridays, he'd have a weekend pass. MaryAnn gave him news of the family.

"Peter Jr.'s on his way overseas—Europe, probably. Mari was devastated when Johnny left. She wandered around the house for a week like a little lost soul."

"How's the queen? How's Helen?"

"Deflated. It's hard to hold court when the subjects are being shipped out one by one."

"Nobody's left?"

"Nobody. Well, Willie Churlin. He's Four-F. Mama told Helen that Willie's been asking about her. Bettie thinks he wants her to go out with him."

"No kidding? The fat guy at the store? What'd Helen say?"

"In a pig's eye! That's what she said."

They laughed and walked around until, one by one, the lights behind the blackout curtains along the streets blinked off. Rick took MaryAnn back to the hotel, and her last sight of him was running for all he was worth to catch the last bus back to camp.

MaryAnn woke up late the next morning. She came downstairs looking for some coffee.

"Dining room's already closed for breakfast," the woman behind the desk told her. "But go on in. I'm sure I can find some coffee in the kitchen. You need anything else? Toast, maybe?"

"Coffee's fine," she answered gratefully.

The woman returned with two steaming cups. "Your name's MaryAnn, right?" She handed over one of them. "I remembered from the register. Mine's Effie."

"Thank you, Effie," MaryAnn spooned a sugar cube into her cup from the glass dish on the table.

"Mind if I sit? Things are slow at the desk right now."

"I'd like the company," MaryAnn said, stirring her coffee. "This is such a homey place. I like it a lot."

"It's got character," Effie edged a lone crumb off the table. "But I've been here so long, I hardly notice anymore. My husband and I bought the place and fixed it up years ago. We ran it together until he passed on. Then I sold out. Told the new owners I'd keep on at the desk if they'd hire me, and they agreed. Keeps me occupied."

"I'm sorry that your husband's passed on."

"No need to be. He drank, you see. No sense hidin' it. Anybody in town'll tell you. But in between bouts, that man could work! Why, he could repair almost anything."

"My father … my father drank too," MaryAnn confided.

"Not much to recommend living with someone like that, is there? Sad to say, but I found it easier when my man was gone."

"I hated it, too. I couldn't wait to get away from … well, from the way things were at home." MaryAnn had never said these things to anyone, but she felt a kinship with this leathery old woman who spoke so frankly to her. "So, I got married. That's no reason to marry someone, is it, Effie? It's a terrible reason. But the way things turned out, I'm glad now. I'm so very glad!"

"Well, from what I can tell, you've found yourself a fine young man."

"Oh, yes! Yes, I have! I've been very lucky."

"Hogwash! You picked him, didn't you? Seems to me we make our own luck more often than we give ourselves credit for. Pity I didn't realize it sooner."

"Well, you can change some things," MaryAnn said with spirit, "Like getting away from a bad situation. But you take other things … things like this war for instance … how can anyone change that? Rick's going away. There's even a chance I might never see him again. You know, before these past two months, I never realized how terribly you could miss someone."

"Well, I'd agree with you there. War's different. With war, you just don't get a vote."

"No, you don't! I just pushed it out of my mind at first … the war. I thought we'd find a way to stay out of it. Because what I'd found was so wonderful, so unexpected, I just wanted to hold onto it, to have a normal life … a baby."

"There'll be time for that, honey," the woman said kindly.

"If we had a baby, it's like I could keep Rick with me. It's like he'd be here, no matter what."

"I say you shouldn't take on anything like that now, not if you could avoid it. Raising a child alone is not a good thing to do."

That's what Rick had told her soon after he'd been drafted. He'd wanted to use protection.

"A condom? We can't use condoms. We're Catholic!"

"For God's sake, MaryAnn! There's a war on! We should have used something right away. I hope it's not too late. Besides, I want to be with you when you have our baby. I want to take care of you. Both of you."

"It doesn't matter anyway. I've seen Doc Wimmer. Doc said I have a problem and can't get pregnant, anyway."

"What problem? Do you mean we'll never have a kid?"

"Of course we will, silly. Doc says he can take care of things when you come back. Meanwhile, everything's fine."

"Take care of what? MaryAnn, is this something serious?"

She kept her voice light. "I love you, Rick. I'd tell you if there was anything serious. "

"And there's no chance of you getting pregnant right now? Really?"

"I told you what Doc said." The lie had come easily. What Doc had really told her was that getting pregnant would be more difficult. Her uterus was tipped. That's why they'd gone ten months already. And it was possible she'd never conceive. But Doc went on to say he had delivered babies to women just like her. Sometimes, it just took longer. MaryAnn only had twelve more days. She hoped it would be enough.

"You are a fox," Rick said later that night when they were together again. "Who would have thought the shy girl I married would turn into such a passionate woman? I must be the luckiest guy in the world."

"I'm lucky, too," she smiled. "Besides, we make our own luck more often than we give ourselves credit for."

The rest of their time together was idyllic. MaryAnn met Rick's friends from the base, and she found two other wives who were staying in a rooming house up the street. They spent a few afternoons together, looking around town and chatting. But in the evenings, she and Rick preferred quiet dinners and long walks around the town and in the countryside.

"When I get back, we'll build our own house," Rick promised her. "I can do most of the work myself. I've had experience remodeling our tavern, so building a house won't be anything I can't handle."

"I'd love a home of our own. White. With green shutters in front."

"But I think you should move back home for now, MaryAnn. I know your parents wouldn't mind. There's no way we can afford the place we're in on my Army pay and your salary."

MaryAnn had known all along she'd have to give up the little house. Mama had already told her Papa could fix up their downstairs to make a small apartment for her. She'd have her privacy, Mama said, and could still come upstairs whenever she felt like it. Fixing the apartment would be good for Papa, Mama told her. Keep him busy.

"I hate to give up our place," she said.

"I know. But we can't swing it. And I'd feel better if you weren't all by yourself while I'm gone."

So MaryAnn agreed to move back home.

When the two weeks were up, Rick shipped out to an unknown destination.

MaryAnn boarded the bus home with a heavy heart. She sat drinking in one last look at her first mountains, at the purples, greens, and golds that stippled their peaks. *How could she ever part with this place and her beloved Rick?* MaryAnn laid a light hand on her stomach. *Perhaps, just perhaps, their parting wouldn't be quite so wrenching after all.*

On Leave from Boot Camp – Peter Jr.

When eight weeks were up, Peter Jr. came home on leave. Mari couldn't believe how handsome he looked in his uniform.

"What's that on your sleeve?" Papa wanted to know.

"Private first class."

"A promotion? You got a promotion already?" Mama was beaming.

She made all of Peter Jr.'s favorite foods, and they listened to what it was like in basic training. Besides marching and handling a rifle, Peter Jr. had learned to make a bed with corners so tight a quarter would bounce on it. He discovered he had a knack for typing (60 words a minute) and how to take shorthand. "I'm a clerk," he told them, "They finally saw how bad my eyes were. I couldn't fool them this time around."

"Why do you have a rifle if you're not going to fight?" Mari asked. "Because it's war, half-pint. I'll fight if I have to."

"Will we have to fight here, too?"

"I hope not. That's why I'll go overseas—to stop old Hitler or Tojo before they can get over here."

Mari felt a shiver down her spine. She hoped Peter Jr. would never use his gun.

Peter Jr. didn't know where he would be sent. He wouldn't know until he got his orders. He slept late in the mornings after going out with his friends the night before, those who were still at home. He started staying out later and later, and while Mama and Papa exchanged looks, they didn't say anything about it. One night, Mari awoke to hear a loud bump and a crash from the front room.

"Damn." It was Junior's voice. He was trying to sneak in again. "Cuckoo! Cuckoo! Cuckoo!"

"One of these days, I'm going to shoot that damn bird!"

Mari covered her head with her blanket and giggled into her pillow. The next morning, she had to tell someone what she'd heard. MaryAnn was already gone, so she went looking for Helen. She found her in her room getting ready for work.

"In my arms, in my arms,

Ain't I never going get a girl in my arms.
In my arms, in my arms,
Ain't I never going get a bundle of charms.
Comes the dawn, I'll be gone.
I just gotta have a honey holding me tight."

With Dick Haymes crooning from the Victrola in the background, Mari told Helen about last night.

"Serves him right," Helen sniffed. "Mama and Papa never let any of us girls stay out that late."

"It's because he'll be going overseas," Mari said solemnly. "It's because he's going to war."

Helen said it didn't make any difference. Boys always got to do more things than girls. Hadn't Peter Jr. gone on a trip across the whole United States with two of his friends? Why, he had even lived for a short time in New York City. Helen guessed she'd have to get married before she could live anywhere else. "Unless I was Bettie, of course. Bettie will always do whatever she makes up her mind to do. And Lord help any one of us who tries to stop her."

Right before Peter Jr.'s leave was up, he got his orders. "I'm heading for the East Coast," he said, "so it looks like I could be on my way to Germany." Mari was relieved, but she couldn't say why. When Peter Jr. offered to take her downtown later that afternoon, she was excited. One last look at the old town, he said. So after school, they walked up and down the shopping district together, looking in the store windows and passing the time. When they had a Coke at Kresge's Dime Store, the girl sitting at the counter kept looking at Peter Jr. Just then, Dick Haymes' voice popped into Mari's head,

"You can keep your knittin' and purlin'
If I'm gonna go to Berlin
Gimme a girl in my arms tonight."

They got their picture taken in the photo booth at Neisner's. Crowding in together, Peter pulled the curtain, and they put on big smiles. There were three clicks, and pictures came out of a slot on the wall. Peter Jr. picked one out and put it in his wallet. Mari swallowed hard when he said he would keep it with him all the time. He gave Mari the other two pictures to put in her room.

When she came home from school the next day, Peter was gone. Mari knelt beside her bed that night. "Dear God, please let Peter Jr. be all right. Please don't let him get killed." She thought about all the other people who must be praying right now. She thought about Mama, who always prayed for her parents. Katya hadn't heard from them in a long time. Mari knew Mama prayed every day for news that Grandma and Grandpa were alive. Why hadn't God answered her prayers?

North Africa: Peter's Journal

I was a clerk for a colonel when they yanked me out of the office and told me they needed more men at the front. They sent me to radio school, where I learned Morse code. Soon afterward, I was on a troopship overseas to England. On the voyage across the Atlantic, somebody handed me my paycheck. I knew then that I'd have to show up for work.

The Brits were really nice to us. The way we'd get a date is to walk out at night and try to pick up a girl. It was always pitch-black outside because of the air raids. One night, I could make out a girl's shape up ahead, so I came up beside her and slipped my arm around her waist. She didn't resist and we just kept walking like we'd known each other forever. "Got a cigarette, Yank?" Her voice was throaty. I stopped and pulled a smoke out of my pack, and our hands touched when she took it. When I lit the match, I could see she was pretty. We made a date to meet the next night, but I shipped out the next morning.

Our first stop was Oran, Algeria, while others went to Casablanca. Our missions varied. Sometimes we dropped paratroopers. The Brits were surprised to see us dropping paratroopers below them. British planes flew higher because they didn't have snap chutes to keep the shroud lines on the parachutes from tangling.

Other times, we landed cargo support for commando raids. Once, we delivered land mines so that our troops could salt the ground and slow a German advance. The fields all around us were on fire, and there was a lot of gunfire. I handed out the mines to the GI Joes in the field. We couldn't wait to get out of there.

All I remember about Arab towns was the smell. There was always a big hole just outside of town where inhabitants threw their waste. The smell permeated the air. Some of the later towns used the gutters as toilets. Stink and heat, that was North Africa.

We went from Oran to Thiersville, which was still in Algeria. When we came upon an abandoned German tank, all shot up and left in the desert to rust, Harold, our resident genius, fixed it up. We used it as a truck to haul our stuff to our next stop, Relizane. Harold always had a scheme. Shame he got caught later stealing radio equipment from the Allies. He was selling it to the Arabs, who turned around and sold it to the Germans.

We slept in two-man pup tents until we got to Relizane, where we slept in our first barracks, a Foreign Legion encampment with sandstone walls. Had toilets then, a hole in the floor with footholds on each side. There were dark finger marks on the toilet walls because the Foreign Legion had no toilet paper. The walls were disgusting.

Bathing meant our monthly trip to the Mediterranean Sea. God, that felt good. Water is scarce here. It comes in Lyster bags, big canvas bags (always sweating) hung out in the field. Water is never cold, just wet. We wash our clothes in gasoline flown into us in 50-gallon drums. And it is high test, none of that cheap stuff. Did you know when you wash your skivvies in gasoline long enough, they will turn a dirty gray? We hang them on the plane wing in the sun, and the smell really isn't too bad after a while.

Then there were the little wars within the big war. Sometimes I was attached to British units; the Brits wouldn't let Jews fight because Brits were allies with the Arabs. The Irish are neutral because they hate the Brits more than they hate the Germans. My friend Herb said maybe that is okay because Ireland provides neutral ground to iron out differences. Makes no sense to me, but anyway, that's what Herb says.

One time, we saved up all our canned milk so they could fly it to Cairo to make ice cream. On the long-awaited day, the truck returned, but the ice cream had way too much salt. One guy ate it and died. Sometimes there is just too much shit in a war. No one should die from eating ice cream, for Crissake.

Whenever we roll into a new town, we make sure to ride on the tops of the trucks. That way, we can peer into the courtyards to try to see the women without their veils. One of my pals, Donovan, and I got drunk one night and climbed over a sultan's wall. We dropped down into a courtyard, and the women started screaming. That's sacrilege, you know, to be seen by a stranger when not wearing a veil. The women were yelling, but I wondered if maybe they really liked the adventure.

The sultan and his man came charging out of the house and aiming guns at us. Guns? Christ, they looked like cannons to me. I hightailed it back over the wall. Donovan had trouble because he was so drunk, but I yanked him out just in time. Back out, Donovan laid back against the wall and doubled up with laughter. "That was close. I wasn't sure we'd get away," he gasped. "We nearly got our asses shot off."

In 1942, the Allies won the second battle of El Alamein, a town in Egypt. British Field Marshal Montgomery finally got the upper hand over German Field Marshal Rommel, and the Axis powers withdrew. Even though El Alamein was no more than a train station with a single building, the Germans and Italians fought hard to keep it. They wanted access to the Suez Canal, the ports in Africa, and the oil of the Middle East. At El Alamein, the war in North Africa finally turned in favor of the Allies, boosting Great Britain's spirits. But the Axis had salted the whole area with land mines, so riding across it was still treacherous.

From Algiers, my group went to Tunis, the capital of Tunisia, to wait for the Sicily invasion off the coast of Italy. I was in the Sicily invasion, then went to Sorrento to drop paratroopers. I then went to Rome—well, actually to Brindisi—southeast of Rome.

A Dark Menace

Sinister shadows hammered at the glass again and again until a thick, ugly crack zigzagged across the storefront window. The words "Weise's Sweets" splintered to smithereens. Then brushes slapped, slapped Nazi symbols, big black swastikas, over the mangled glass. "Be quick. Before someone hears us," *a voice whispered. Footsteps faded. Once again, the street was dark and quiet.*

September 24, 1942, was a Saturday morning so bright that you couldn't even see the coal dust hanging in the air. Mari was whistling as she finished wiping the grime from the windowsill in the front room. Soot from the steel mill, but mostly from the nearby coke plant where Papa worked, built up on the sills every day. He joked that when you couldn't see the air you breathed, you couldn't trust it, but on cloudy days, that soot always made his asthma worse.

Mari finished her chores and threw the soiled rags into the laundry basket. She scooped her long brown hair into a ponytail, gulped a peanut butter sandwich and milk, and headed out the door to her friend Sylvia's. Halfway down the block, the sun streamed into Mrs. Trudis's front window, highlighting the gold star hanging there. Mari hated looking at that star. Casmir Trudis joined the army a year ago, the same time as Mari's brother, Johnny, but Casmir had been killed just two months ago. Mrs. Trudis hung the star in her window to remind them all of her son's sacrifice, but all Mari could think about when she saw it was Johnny.

Turning away from the dreaded gold star in the window, Mari remembered Sylvia. She rubbed a thumb over the comforting dime in her pocket and ran all the rest of the way to the candy store.

She paused, out of breath, and that's when she saw it, the broken window splashed with Nazi symbols and paint streaked all the way down to the sidewalk.

Mari's stomach cramped, and a sour taste rose inside her throat. She ran to the store and rattled the doorknob. Locked.

Through the shattered glass, she could make out big jars of Tootsie Rolls, jujubes, jawbreakers, and other colorful candies that were untouched along the narrow counter.

Sylvia! Where was Sylvia?

Muffled sounds came from somewhere, but the street was empty. Running around the side of the building, Mari found Sylvia huddled cross-legged on the grass. She hugged herself, shivering even though it was a warm autumn day.

"You saw? You saw what they did?" she sobbed.

"Oh, Sylvia. I did. But who would do such a terrible thing?"

She rubbed a sleeve under her nose and looked at Mari through red, puffy eyes, "We don't know. Grandma called the police."

"Did they come?"

"A policeman came and looked around. He talked with a man and a woman down the street, but they said they didn't see anything."

"Nothing? Nobody suspicious?"

"No. Then another policeman came, and he went around the neighborhood, too. But the people he talked to didn't see anything, either."

"Do you have any idea who it could be?"

"None. But people avoid us on the street, and others turn their heads when they pass by the store. And Grandma said some boys came inside yesterday and told her that real Americans don't buy things from Germans."

"Your grandma's German?"

"Oh, Mari, they called her a Kraut. They made fun of the way she talks."

"Well, people on my block have accents, too," Mari said, trying to make
sense of what was happening. "They came from different countries to work in the mill."

"Are they German, too?"

"I'm not sure," she answered uncertainly. It was a problem she'd never considered before. The Germans she knew about were in the war movies at the Tivoli Theater uptown. Those

Germans were mean and carried guns. They looked at you through sneaky eyes. Mrs. Weise was just a grandma who sold candy.

They sat on the grass for a long time, Sylvia looking glum and Mari racking her brain for some way to help. "Let's go get some chips, Sylvia," Mari said, holding up her dime. "My treat."

On Saturday mornings, kids would go across town and cut through an alley to the back door of the Peerless Potato Chip Factory. They rang the bell, and a lady in a hairnet and a crisp white uniform opened the door. For a nickel, she handed out a warm bag of chips. The smell of potatoes bubbling in hot oil always made their mouths water, and the tall bag of chips lasted most of the way back to the store.

But Sylvia shook her head. Today, not even her favorite treat could coax her out of her misery. She just slumped on the ground, plucking at the sparse tufts of grass around her. It was like that all morning, and the hours seemed to drag on forever.

When the mill whistle signaled noon, Mrs. Weise poked her head out the door of the tiny apartment above the store. *"Komm her und iss dein Mittagessen, Silvie."*

"Grandma says it's lunchtime," Sylvia said and squeezed Mari's hand before heading up the stairs.

Mari rose and brushed the grass from her pants. Around the corner, a battered pickup truck carrying ladders and long planks of lumber chugged up to the curb in front of the store. Two burly men climbed out and began hauling long planks of wood onto the sidewalk.

"What are you doing?" Mari asked.

"Cops called us. The old lady said to board up the window."

Mari watched them for a while and then turned toward home.

Hotsy Totsy

In class on Monday morning, Mari kept trying to get Sylvia's attention, but Sylvia wouldn't look up from her desk.

"Recess!" Donald yelled, pushing past Mari into the cloakroom and grabbing his jacket off the hook. "Wait up, Lon!"

On nice days, most fifth graders played dodgeball or Red Rover in the schoolyard, but those two spent all their free time playing war.

"Today, we're infantry!" Donald poked his finger into Lon's pudgy stomach. "Get ready to mow down the Japs, Lon! Let's make 'em pay for sneaking up on us at Pearl Harbor!"

"And the Germans, Don! I say we kill all the dirty Germans!" He dropped to his knees and waved an imaginary machine gun around the playground. "Brrrrrrrrrr."

"I'm German." Sylvia thrust out her jaw and stood with her fists clenched.

"Germans are killers!" Lon scowled. "They want to take over the world and kill everybody."

"Not all Germans. Most Germans are good people."

"They're not!" Donald cried.

Lon turned his imaginary gun on Sylvia. "Brrrrrrrrrr."

She didn't flinch. She just stood with her shoulders hunched and her head down like a bulldog.

"What are you doing? Let's get out of here!" Mari grabbed Sylvia's arm and pulled her away.

Sylvia shrugged her off and ran to the merry-go-round. She waved Mari to a seat. "My grandma is a good, kind person. It's not right that she has to close her store just because she's German."

"She's closing the store? But why?"

"Because she's afraid something worse than a broken window could happen next time."

"Hotsy totsy, Sylvia's a Nazi!" Lon and Donald shouted.

Mari jumped onto the wooden bench of the merry-go-round and swung her legs to the center. "Don't pay attention to them," she called as she grabbed the metal bar.

101

Sylvia took hold of the bench and pushed, running alongside the merry-go-round and kicking up dust as the ride picked up speed. Finally, she jumped up next to Mari, swung her legs to the center, and reached for the bar. Together, they worked it back and forth.

Out of the corner of her eye, Mari could see Sylvia's hair flying around her face as they pushed and pulled faster and faster until the mocking faces blurred and the only sound was the rushing wind. Round and round they went until Sylvia's mouth relaxed and she smiled at Mari, who smiled, too.

Suddenly, the ride jerked and slowed down. The boys were dragging them to a halt! Sylvia jumped off to push again, but Lon cut in front of her and shoved his piggy little face into hers. He bumped her hard with his stomach. Mari could see the pain in Sylvia's face as the bell signaled recess was over. She grabbed Sylvia's hand, and they squeezed past the boys and ran back to the schoolhouse.

When the final bell of the day rang, Mari looked around for Sylvia, but she was already gone. Lon and Donald were planted on either side of the outside door, waiting. Mari pulled her shoulders back, eyes straight ahead, and barreled past them.

"Hotsy totsy, Mari's a Nazi."

"Stop it!" she cried, eyes blazing. "I'm not a Nazi. Neither is Sylvia! She's just worried about her grandma."

"Her grandma?"

"Mrs. Weise," she blurted. "Somebody broke Mrs. Weise's store window and painted swastikas all over the front. She has to close her store. Sylvia's worried about her grandma."

"So, Mrs. Weise's a Kraut? Well, whaddaya know!"

Mari's heart sank. She'd made it worse! How could she think those two would care about Sylvia, her grandma, or anyone else, for that matter? *Fat chance,* she thought, and ran out of the building, not slowing down until her sides hurt. She was panting when she reached her front gate.

She found Mama in the garden behind the house, picking beans. "The last batch for this year," she said and hefted herself to her feet. "But we did well with our first Victory

Garden. Last year, when President Roosevelt asked citizens to plant gardens, I went out the next day and bought seeds. Growing our own food means farmers can grow more for the troops overseas—troops like Johnny."

"Papa showed me the newspaper pictures of the big garden behind the White House. Mrs. Roosevelt is holding a giant squash. She said that we all need to do our part for the war effort."

"I just hope what we're doing will bring Johnny home sooner," Mama sighed. She handed Mari the pan filled with beans. "Your face is flushed, Mari. Is anything wrong?"

"It's Lon and Donald, two boys from school. They followed me. I had to run home."

"Are you all right?"

"Sure. I'm faster than they are."

"Why did they chase you?"

"Because Sylvia told them she's German, and I'm her best friend. I don't know why she told them that!"

"You said Sylvia was born in this country."

"She was. But her grandmother came from Germany."

"Except for the native Indians, all American families started somewhere else."

"But they won't stop calling us names."

"You know, Mari, these days, people are afraid. They're suspicious, sometimes for the wrong reasons. In California, they took Japanese families out of their homes and put them in internment camps, panicking that they wanted to hurt our country. Around here, people don't speak German to their children anymore. Even Rick's family is careful not to use any German words in their tavern. Someone might overhear and think they are Nazis."

"Rick's family? But he's an American soldier!" Mari said, thinking of the sandy-haired boy who loved to tease her. "He's overseas fighting for our country! How could anyone think Rick's family are Nazis?"

"People don't trust each other anymore. This war is like an infection threatening to poison us all." She caught herself and smiled. "Don't worry. It will soon be over, and everything will be all right." But Mari could tell her heart wasn't in her smile.

Back at her desk the next day, Mari was opening her writing workbook when a shrill noise pierced the air.

"Into the hall, class! It's an air raid drill," their teacher commanded.

Mari could feel the hairs on the back of her neck stand up. Drills were only supposed to take place at night! At home, she always looked at the clock when the siren wailed to make sure it was eight o'clock. But here was her teacher, Mrs. Martin, striding to the front of the room. "Because this is wartime, there is a chance we could have an air raid while we are at school."

Please let it be a drill, she prayed, *only a drill.*

At Churlin's Grocery Store, Willie Churlin was always talking about the mill pumping out steel for guns and ammunition. It was a prime target for German bombers, and it wasn't far away.

"While our defenses would certainly shoot down any enemy bombers before they could get here," Mrs. Martin was saying, "we must be prepared." The siren cut the air again as they marched in a line into the hallway.

Sitting on the floor with her back to the wall, Mari drew her legs up and put her head on her knees the way Mrs. Martin had taught them. Turning her head, she could see the long, anxious row of children crouched together. The sharp wail hurt her ears. *I just want to go home,* she thought miserably.

"Dirty Krauts," Lon hissed.

Finally, the all-clear sounded, and they went back to class. Mari was relieved, glad to be back in the room where the colors on the bulletin board looked brighter and more cheerful than usual. She felt lucky to open her workbook and have her stomach settling back to normal. Everyone was quiet for the rest of the morning. Even Lon kept his remarks to himself for a change.

But later, the boys followed them onto the playground. Donald came over and pushed his face close to Sylvia's.

"My old man says the only good German is a dead German."

Sylvia's face crumpled, and she fled in tears to the bathroom. When Lon spun to run after her, Mari stuck her foot out, and he skidded headlong into the dirt. When he stood up, madder than a hornet, his nose was bleeding, and his face, except for two circles around his eyes, was covered with dirt. He looked like a raccoon. Heart pounding, she planted her feet, ready for him.

"Lon, what's happened to you?" Mrs. Martin cried, hurrying over.

Oh, no, Mari winced. *I'm in trouble now.*

But she squared her shoulders and looked her teacher in the eye.

"Lon and Donald keep calling Sylvia and me Nazis, Mrs. Martin. Sylvia's grandma is German, and Lon said the only good German is a dead German. I wanted to stop them."

"Come inside, Lon. Let's get you cleaned up. I need to talk to you and Donald anyway. I've been watching you the past few days." And she marched them back to the schoolhouse.

They weren't waiting at the door after school, and Mari skipped most of the way home, looking back only once to make sure they weren't following. School was peaceful after that. Lon and Donald would slink off by themselves to the far corner of the playground when the bell rang for recess. The other kids ignored them. Maybe, Mari thought, they didn't like imaginary guns pointing at them, either.

More Troubles

"Sylvia must really be sick, Mrs. Martin. She hasn't been at school all week."

"Yes, I'm concerned about her too, Mari. I know it's out of your way, but could you swing by her apartment on your way home? It would help if you could drop off her homework. I hate to see her getting so far behind."

"Sure," Mari said, only too glad for an excuse to see Sylvia for even a few minutes. It was lonely without her. After school, she got the books out of Sylvia's desk and waited for Mrs. Martin to mark her homework.

"Tell her we all hope she gets well soon. If her grandmother thinks she's going to be out much longer, I'll send Miss Henderson to check on her." Miss Henderson was the school nurse. Sometimes she examined the kids for head lice; last year, two kids had to go home and have their heads doused with kerosene.

After school, Donald was showing Lon a picture he'd torn from a magazine. "It's the P-fifty-one Mustang fighter plane. It carries six machine guns!" Just then, he spied Mari and aimed his imaginary gun at her. "Brrrrrr. Goodbye, Nazi."

"Creep!" Mari fired back and headed to the candy store. Wondering how a few extra books could feel so heavy, she quickened her step so she wasn't too late getting home. Mama would wonder what had happened to her.

The store was still boarded up, and as she got closer, she saw the ugly swastikas still visible through the thin layer of paint meant to cover them up. She went to the back of the building, climbed the long flight of stairs, and knocked.

"Won't do you no good, girlie. They're gone." A gnarled old man was eyeing her from the foot of the stairs.

"Did you say something?"

"I said the old lady and the girl are gone. Vamoosed. I watched 'em come downstairs with their suitcases."

"When?"

"Couple days ago. Friday, I guess it was."

"Do you know where they went?

106

"I couldn't say," he said, spitting tobacco juice into the grass. "Just as well, if you ask me. Their kind aren't exactly welcome in the neighborhood."

"What kind is that?" Mari asked uncertainly.

"Krauts. Both the old lady and the girl. Strange pair. They keep to themselves. Don't neighbor around like the rest of the folks."

"Somebody broke their window. That's why they don't—"

"Now, you take the old lady. She's some piece of work. Shifty eyes. German accent so thick you could slice it with a knife." He looked around quickly. "Rumor has it that she could be a spy."

"Mrs. Weise?" Mari pictured the frail woman behind the candy counter. "Why would you think Mrs. Weise is a spy?"

"Say, who are you, anyway? Why are you trying to get in there?"

"I'm Mari, and Sylvia is my friend. And you'd better watch out how you talk about people!" She clutched the books to her chest and clambered back down the stairs, glaring at the old man and pushing past him before she ran down the street toward home.

"Sylvia's gone!" Mari burst into the kitchen, dropping her books on the table. "I stopped by to bring her homework, and an old man told me they left last Friday. They came down the stairs with suitcases."

"They might have gone to visit relatives."

"Sylvia never talked about any relatives."

"What about her parents? Did she ever say anything about them? Are they living?"

"They must be. Once when I asked why she lived with her grandma, she said her parents were away but would be sending for her soon."

"Well, that could explain it. She could be on her way to them right now."

Mari's heart sank. She didn't want to lose Sylvia. Before she came, there was no one to spend Saturdays with, share secrets with, or choose when they played Red Rover at recess.

She couldn't imagine the rest of the year without Sylvia. "I'm worried, Mama."

"I'm sure there's a simple explanation, Mari. Tomorrow morning, just be sure to talk to Mrs. Martin. The school will surely know how to contact her relatives."

Sylvia wasn't at school the next day, and when Mari told Mrs. Martin what happened when she tried to deliver her homework, the teacher frowned and hurried away to the office. Later when she asked if there was any news, Mrs. Martin just smiled her reassuring smile. "Not yet. But I'm sure everything will be fine."

Sylvia didn't show up for the rest of the week, either. On Friday after school, Mari decided to cut through the alley on her way home. She was on the lookout for scrap metal. Neighbors left old pans, small appliances, and tools (once she found a hubcap) beside their trash barrels to be melted down for guns and ammunition. There was a scrap drive at school every month, and Mari's room was ahead in points. She wanted to keep it that way.

The alley on her block was paved and mostly tidy, everywhere but behind Edith Fleming's house. Edith lived across the alley, and her barrel was always packed tight and overflowing with newspapers and other papers in different languages. On windy days, neighbors complained about the papers blowing helter-skelter up and down the pavement. How, they asked, could one person read so many newspapers?

But Mari liked Edith, who treated her more like a grownup than any of the other adults. Mama said Edith was the smartest person in the neighborhood—maybe in the whole town. She was a college graduate, which was a rare thing for a woman. Edith told Mama that Mari should go to college, but Papa said college was a waste of time for a woman and that she wouldn't need a fancy education to keep house for her husband.

Whispering Voices

Looking over the fence into Edith's yard, Mari saw the house's back curtains part. When she raised her hand to wave, the curtain dropped quickly, but not before Mari knew she had been looking not at Edith but right straight at Sylvia.

She ran through the back gate and made a beeline for the house. Bounding up the steps, she pounded on the door.

"I saw you, Sylvia! Edith, let me in!"

The door opened, and Edith took her by the arm and yanked her into the house. "Be quiet, Mari. What are you doing here, anyway?"

Sylvia was standing next to the stove with her grandma at her back. The kitchen floor was unusually clean, not covered with newspapers because of Edith's many cats. Even the counters were bare, clear of the open tins of cat food usually lined up there. By some miracle, the cats were gone, too, all except a tiny kitten that came up purring to rub against her leg.

"Everyone's been worried sick about you, Sylvia. About both of you. What are you doing here?"

Sylvia shrank back and seemed to fold into herself. "They're here because they're afraid," Edith said.

"Afraid of what?"

"Afraid of the people calling them on the telephone."

"Bad people," Sylvia said softly. "Grandma said we had to go away again."

"Again?" This wasn't getting any clearer. "Who's calling you?"

"We don't know, child. Voices. Whispering voices."

"What did they say?"

"They said Germans must be punished. They … said …" Mrs. Weise ran a hand across her eyes. "Oh, what does it matter? I knew they wanted to hurt us."

"Did you call the police?"

"Police!" she spat. "I called your police when those hooligans broke my window and painted swastikas on the building. What good did it do?"

"But why did you come here?"

"We came because we know Edith from synagogue. We trust her."

"What's 'synagogue'?"

"It's like your church," Edith told Mari. "It's like St. Michael's."

"Why do they go there?"

"Because they're Jews."

Mari tried to understand, but every answer only seemed to bring more questions.

"I'm sorry you've been worried about Sylvia," Edith said kindly. "You're a good friend."

But was she? She remembered the first time she saw Sylvia standing beside Mrs. Martin's desk, a tall girl, awkward and shy.

"Class, this is Sylvia Kaplan, a new student. I hope you will all make her feel welcome. Mari, I thought you might be able to show her around and help her get acquainted."

By the end of the week, they were best friends. But now, Mari realized there was still a lot to learn about Sylvia Kaplan.

"Well, you can't go on hiding," Mari told them. "You must call the police."

"Nein! Keine Polizei mehr! No police. I have dealt with them too many times."

"But you said you didn't call them," Mari protested.

"Not here. In Germany!" It came out *Churmany.*

"It's been very hard for them," Edith said.

Mrs. Weise sat down heavily. "We have come such a long distance, child, only to find that nothing changes. Sylvia's mother is my daughter. When she married, she followed her husband to America. He came here to study. They came to love America, so after her husband finished graduate school, they decided to stay here for good. A year later, Sylvia was born. I missed them and was very sad.

"The years passed, and I got terribly sick. I wrote to my daughter of my fear that I would not live long enough to see my granddaughter, so they came back to Germany to care for me. My recovery was long, much longer than anyone expected, and life for our people grew worse by the day.

Sylvia's father struggled to make a living and was hard-pressed to scrape up enough money to survive."

"But why? What did he do?"

"It's not what he did," Mrs. Weise said sadly. "It's what he was. A Jew. Sylvia's parents knew there was no future for them in Germany, but they were not allowed to leave. So, we decided to devise a plan to get Sylvia out. Since I had money hidden away, I applied for a visa, a small trip to celebrate my granddaughter's birthday. What could be the harm in that?

"After a time, I actually got the documents, and we ran. When we got out, we just kept going. Friends helped us. Sometimes they hid us. Finally, when we got to Holland, they helped us get to America. They said we would be safe here." She laughed bitterly.

"But where are Sylvia's parents?" Mari asked.

Mrs. Weise sighed. "We don't know."

"You haven't heard from them?"

"Nothing. Not one word." Mrs. Weise's voice broke, and her eyes clouded over. She'd retreated to some far-off place behind her eyes, someplace they couldn't follow.

Edith said, "Four years ago, a mob of Hitler's thugs, the Brownshirts, stormed across Germany. They smashed the windows of Jewish businesses and beat up the people. Overnight, Germany was a police state."

"Not even an ant can escape now," Sylvia said mournfully.

"I told her that it's different here," Edith protested. "The government, the police aren't the same as in the old country."

"She's right, Bubbi." Smiling gently, Sylvia took her grandmother's hand and led her to the telephone.

"Operator," Mrs. Weise said, her voice strong now, "connect me with the police."

When Mrs. Weise replaced the receiver, they could read the relief written on her face. "I spoke with Sgt. Pulver, the policeman who came to the store after the window was broken. He said the police would listen in on our telephone to find out who's making those nasty calls. And," she added in disbelief, "he and his partner have been checking the store every night."

111

Before long, Sylvia and her grandma were back in their own apartment, and Sylvia was back in school.

"Vas is dis?" Lon hissed as Sylvia took her seat. "Again, the Churmans haf landed?"

Donald thought it was all very funny until Mrs. Martin smacked her ruler down on his desk. "That's enough, Donald!"

Heads shot up. The kids had never seen Mrs. Martin like this. "Lon! I never want to hear talk like that again!"

When the bell rang for recess, Sylvia made a dash for the door. Mari ran to catch up, but Sylvia had already pushed past Donald and was zeroed in on Lon.

"It was you, wasn't it?"

"What?"

"On the telephone. Lon, I know it was you."

"What's happening here?" Mrs. Martin must have seen Sylvia with Lon because she came up right away.

"It's him, Mrs. Martin. On the telephone. I recognize his voice now."

"What about the telephone?"

"They called us. Whispering voices. They said they would punish us. They would hurt my grandma," said Sylvia. "Is that true, Lon?"

Lon turned to Donald for help, but he looked away and was suddenly busy digging a toe into the dirt.

"I don't know what she's talking about," Lon said, shifting uneasily.

"Look at me, Lon! I want the truth."

His face melted like soft butter. "It was just a joke, Mrs. Martin. We didn't mean anything. Donald and me, we just thought we'd have a little fun."

"Into the principal's office! Both of you! March!"

112

A Fine Piece of Meat

The next morning, there was a police car in front of the school building. When the bell rang, Mrs. Martin rose from her desk. "Leave your books in your desks for now. First, I'm sure you've all noticed the patrol car parked out in front when you came inside. The police have been called to investigate the property destruction, threats, and intimidation that have been taking place in our neighborhood. The police tell us they will find the lawbreakers, and they will be punished."

Mari looked back behind her. Lon and Donald were not in their seats. Mrs. Martin continued, "We are at war, and our troops are fighting overseas so that all nations can live in freedom. What does that mean, to be free? Your parents and your grandparents knew. That's why they came here from many different countries to build a new country, a country with a better idea. With their different skills, dress, languages, and religious beliefs, they came to a land where they could live without fear. They came because they wanted to be free.

"Look around the room, class. Who do you see? Do you see Swedes or Syrians, Irish or English, Italians, Serbs, Germans?" Mari looked around at Sylvia and then at the other kids; the way Mrs. Martin put it, it was like seeing every kid for the very first time.

"Let me tell you what I see. I see Americans. Our differences are our strengths; if we turn on one another, hurt each other, destroy our neighbors' property, then we are no better than our enemies."

Mari liked what Mrs. Martin said.

"But Grandma is still afraid," Sylvia told her later. "She fears bad things can happen again."

Mari walked home with all sorts of ideas swirling in her head. But inside the house, she smelled something heavenly. Pot roast! After dropping her books and her jacket in her room, she ran into the kitchen.

"A fine piece of meat," Mama beamed, raising the lid from the roasting pan she'd pulled out of the oven. Unbelievable, but there it was, a succulent brown roast in a bed of onions, carrots, and potatoes. Mari bent over the pan and inhaled a scent so delicious, it warmed her all the way down to her toes.

"How long since we've sat down to a meal like this?" Mama enthused. "I can't remember the last time I got such a prime cut, what with the rationing and all."

Papa wouldn't be home for a while, but Mari eagerly got to work setting the table. She pulled their special napkins from the side drawer and brought out the pretty pitcher from the cupboard. From the side yard, she cut two yellow asters and placed them in a little glass in the center of the table. Satisfied, she went to do her homework.

After a while, she came back into the kitchen where Mama stood at the sink admiring the maple tree outside the window. "Papa planted it right after Johnny was born," she liked to tell Mari. "Now it keeps me company until he comes back home again."

"I can't study, Mama. I keep thinking about Sylvia. And about her grandma, too. Mrs. Weise is convinced everyone in the neighborhood hates them."

Mama sighed, turned, and took off her apron. "Get your jacket, Mari. Hurry. We haven't much time."

Mari snatched up her coat and ran back to the kitchen. Mama had put on her sweater and two huge oven mitts. Clutching the roaster by its handles, she led the way through the front room, out the door, and down the front steps. When Mama was on a mission, it was all anyone could do to keep up with her. They fairly flew past the neighbors' houses and down the next blocks. Finally, with the little shop in sight, they could see how pitiful it looked all boarded up like that.

They rounded the building and Mama lumbered up the long flight of stairs, flushed but determined to deliver the prize she gripped in her bulky mitts. Mari knocked at the door, but there was no answer. She knocked again, and Mama nodded at her to keep on going. After a very long time, the door opened a crack, and they could see Sylvia peering out.

"Tell your grandmother she has visitors," Mama ordered.

When Mrs. Weise came to the door, Mama practically shoved the roaster into her hands.

"A fine piece of meat," she said to the tiny woman who stood squinting at them in the late afternoon sun. "I was lucky to get it." Suddenly, the wind kicked up, so Mama pulled her sweater tight around her. "I am Katya Cmar. I believe you know Mari. We've come to let you know you have friends in the neighborhood."

For the rest of her life, Mari would remember the expression on Mrs. Weise's face as she looked first at the roaster and then at Mama.

"I … we … would you … would you care to step inside?"

"Another time," Mama smiled. "We'll come back for the pan. Gives us an excuse to come again. Eat now while the food is warm."

"Why did we have to hurry, Mama?"

"Because you eat pot roast before it gets cold. That's what you do with a fine piece of meat."

At the foot of the stairs, Mari saw Sylvia raise her hand in a tiny wave and Mari flashed her a smile. That night, they had macaroni and cheese for supper, and Mari read the end of her Nancy Drew mystery before bed. Later, she thought about Mrs. Weise and about how surprised she looked standing there holding the pot roast. She closed her eyes and smiled. And that night she slept better than she had in a long, long time. Maybe Sylvia did, too.

The Letter

On what should have been a lazy Saturday morning, Mari was up to her armpits in chores. There had been no letter from Johnny in a long time, and Mama was worried. And when Mama was anxious, they cleaned.

"We'll wash the windows."

"We just washed them last Friday, Mama. I was going to Sylvia's. A new girl's coming over, and we were going to show her around the neighborhood."

"Later. After we've finished our work."

"You mean *my* work," Mari grumbled under her breath. She gave the window above the kitchen sink one last swipe before moving into the front room. The winter sky looked threatening when she pulled back the curtain. Maybe they would have snow for Thanksgiving. The weather had been gloomy all week, and Mama's spirit went downhill with each passing day. Mari pulled the curtain further back in time to see the postman rounding the corner. She didn't bother with her coat but raced outside to meet him.

"I think this might be what you're looking for." He smiled and handed over a thin envelope he'd pulled from his pouch. She grinned her thanks and sprinted back up the walk into the house.

"We got a letter!" Mari whooped as the front door slammed behind her.

"I'm upstairs!" Mama called from Johnny's room in the attic. She clattered down the narrow stairs into the kitchen, set down her bucket, and went to wring out her rag in the sink.

"Open it."

Eagerly, Mari tore open the envelope. "It's not much of a letter," she frowned, scanning the page covered with black marks.

Mama wiped her hands and took the paper. "Well, we do know it was cold that day," she sighed, reading the only sentence she could make out. "So, I'm guessing he must be somewhere in Europe. And we got a letter, Mari; the letter is what's important."

Mari knew what Mama meant; even a blank page told them Johnny was alive. At least he was when he sent it.

"We'll send him *rozki,*" Mama beamed. "Mari, run over to Churlin's and get two cakes of yeast. And take the ration book to get our sugar allotment; I've been saving coupons for a long time. If we bake and send them right away, Johnny just might have his favorite pastries for Thanksgiving. Other families might like cookies, but Johnny's favorite has always been my apricot *rozki.*"

"They're my favorite, too," Mari said as she grabbed the coupon book from the drawer and snatched up her coat. She ran to the side gate to cut through the alley. Knees high, she marched.

Company K's a bunch of jerks, parley vous.
Company K's a bunch of jerks, parley vous.
Company K's a bunch of jerks,
They're always gummin' up the works.
Hinky, dinky, parley vous.

"Hold up, Mari! Slow down!" Edith Fleming hurried to catch up. "I thought I'd cut through the alley and save some time. What is that you're singing?"

"A marching song Johnny taught me when he came home from 'basic'," she said, showing off her Army lingo.

"Yes. I remember he did come home on furlough after basic training. Now I assume he's shipped out overseas. Have you heard from him?"

"Sort of. We finally got a letter, but the words are mostly blacked out. We're sending him *rozki.*"

"Katya's Austrian pastries? I'm sure he'll love them."

"They're his favorite."

"Any idea where he is?"

"Mama thinks Europe somewhere."

"Well, I'm on my way to Mrs. Trudis's; the upcoming holidays are proving especially hard for her since she lost her son. Speaking of holidays, I wonder if we'll ever see smoke coming from Churlin's smokehouse again. Oh, how I miss his smoked turkeys."

"And ham. Nothing beats smoked ham. Smoked sausage, too," agreed Mari. They looked mournfully at the unused concrete hut at the back of Churlin's store. Do you think Mr. Churlin will smoke any meat at all this year? Maybe for Thanksgiving?"

"I wish!" Mari yearned. "All we ever eat is Spam."

"Oh, well. There is a war on. Say hello to your mother for me." Edith turned to make her way up the street.

"Johnny's in Company I!" Mari shouted after her, and Edith raised a hand to show she'd heard. Mari turned in the opposite direction and belted out the rest of the song.

Company I's the best of all, parley vous.
Company I's the best of all, parley vous.
Company I's the best of all,
They keep on going till they fall,
Hinky, dinky, parley vous.

"Parade rest!" Mari snapped off a salute and stopped outside Churlin's. The neighborhood grocery on the corner of Thirteenth and Grant faced the busy thoroughfare that was Grant Street, not like the quiet street where Mari lived. The bell over the door tinkled when she went in, but if he heard it, Mr. Churlin didn't open his eyes.

"Good morning, Kresny."

Steve Churlin, called *Kresny* or "Uncle" by the kids in the neighborhood, opened one eye and then closed it again. He sighed and then hunkered further down on the upturned orange crate next to the front window, his favorite seat. His thick arms were crossed over the white butcher's apron that covered his great stomach.

"Radio says a couple of German prisoners escaped from the work farm up near Valparaiso. Citizens are warned to be on the lookout." Kresny's son Willie, in the aisle across the way, was talking over a beefy shoulder to a new customer, a short, gray-haired lady Mari had never seen before. Willie, heavy like Kresny but taller, moved with light steps for a big man. He came back with two cans of green beans and a can of peas and set them on the counter.

"I didn't know we had prisoners around here," the customer said, looking around furtively as though they might appear any minute. She tucked an iron-gray curl back into the soft turban covering her ears.

"Yep. There's some up north and more at the big camp south of here that used to be an army base."

"I can't say I like German prisoners so close."

"Well, I guess we have to put them somewhere."

"Still, I don't like it at all."

"So, Mari, what can I get for you today?" *Kresna* Churlin, or "Auntie," came in through the door that separated the house in back where the Churlins lived from the store itself. She brushed a few crumbs from her noontime sandwich from the bib of her apron and bustled over to the counter.

On the shelf behind her, Kresna's gallstones floated in a jar next to the pork and beans. Before the war, every new customer had to listen to the drama of Kresna's gallbladder operation.

"They rushed me to the hospital in an ambulance," she would say, patting the rigid waves of her beauty shop hairstyle. "Gave me the operation then and there; I was that sick. And these right here, these were the cause!" She waved the jar with a flourish.

"Doctor told me they're the biggest stones he ever saw. Gave 'em to me as a souvenir." She turned the jar so that everyone could admire the gray lumps lazing in their bath. But these days, the jar sat neglected, gathering dust, while customers focus on the bigger drama of war.

"We need two cakes of yeast, Kresna. And sugar. I have the coupon book here somewhere," Mari said, searching her pockets.

"Why do you call her Kresna?" the little lady wanted to know.

"It means Auntie. In Slovak," Kresna said. "I'm Kresna, 'Auntie,' and Kresny over there on the crate is 'Uncle' to the folks in the neighborhood."

Kresny gave a snort, and his second chin slid further down on his chest.

"So you're not really the girl's aunt and uncle?"

"No. People around here come from many different countries. Immigrant children were encouraged to call grownups 'aunt' and 'uncle' to create a sort of family because their own relatives were so far away."

"Especially during the Depression," Willie said. "Ma says hard times brought people closer."

Mari knew that during the Depression, Kresna let Mama pay for their groceries on days when Papa had work. Other times, Kresna would "write it in the book" or keep track of the bill until Mama came back to settle up.

"How's your brother, Mari? Any letters?"

"Got one today. Only line we could read said it was cold."

"He's somewhere in Europe," Willie offered.

"Willie, why haven't you been drafted? Big man like you," asked the little lady.

"I'm Four-F," he replied sadly and pointed to his heart. "Bad ticker."

"That so?" she replied.

"Yeah. Nothing worse than being Four-F. People think you're a coward."

Mari laid out her coupons and then paid for the sugar before heading out the door. She saw that the crate where Kresny had been sitting was empty. When she cut through the alley again, there was the thinnest wisp of smoke trailing from the smokehouse. She sniffed. Could it be? Was there really a faint smell of ham in the air?

She tore up the alley and banged into the house. "Mama! Kresny's smoking hams! Better order one before he tells you there's nothing left."

Mama went for her coat and pocketbook and then headed for the door.

"If he has turkeys, get one for Edith!" she called after her. After she'd gone, Mari went to finish the front room window when she spied the coupons still on the counter.

"Wait up, Mama!"

"Don't flip your lips," Mama chided when Mari handed her the ration book.

120

"Your lid, Mama."

"What?"

"It's your lid."

"What lid?"

"'Don't flip your lid.' That's the expression."

Mama sighed. She worked hard at English, but slang didn't come easy for her.

"Did you get the ham?" Mari wanted to know when she came back home.

"Well, Kresny said he'd save one, but until I hold it in my hand, I won't

believe him," she scowled.

Predicting what Kresny would do was like predicting the weather. It all started with his thumb.

"I couldn't believe it, Peter. He carved out three beautiful pork chops for me that day. Imagine! *Three.* In *wartime!* He waddled over to the scale the way he always does, slapped them down, wrapped them in a flash, and handed them over to me."

"I didn't realize pork was so expensive," I told him when I saw the price he'd marked on the package.

"Wartime." He shrugged and lumbered back to his crate.

"Well, on the way home, something jogged my memory. Weren't there price controls in wartime? That's when his fat pink thumb popped into my head. Did I see him press it down on the scale, or was it my imagination? So from then on, I watched."

Mari was there when things came to a head. Mama bought hot dogs, now called "Victory Sausages," with their meat allowance. Kresny plopped them on the scale. Turning slightly, the way he always did, he blocked her view. But not before she saw his thumb up there on the scale.

"Kresny! Stop!"

Several customers looked over. She raised her thumb in a pantomime and pressed it down. A woman snickered. Another gave her a knowing smile.

Hands on her hips, she glared at him. Even Kresna, behind the front counter, took notice. She issued a tight-lipped hiss, "Steve!"

He harrumphed, stomped to the counter, and wrapped the meat so fast he forgot to mark the price and had to take the package back to mark it again.

"Something wrong over there?" Willie wanted to know.

Kresny glared at Mama, then at everyone else, before he turned and stormed into the house.

"He didn't even apologize," she told Peter afterward.

"I saw the tips of his ears turn pink," said Mari, who'd been watching the whole thing. "So you knew he felt sorry."

"Sorry for being caught," Mama fumed, "not for what he did."

"Steve's a chiseler," Papa admitted, "but he and Anna were good to us during the Depression. Remember that."

"That was Anna's doing, not his. I can't think why she married him in the first place."

Katya went to the pantry for cookie sheets while Mari hunted for the lard. "I want to get these *rozki* baked, packaged, and sent before supper. There's a blood drive at the Red Cross, and I want to get there before they close."

Later, Mari hurried to the post office to mail the package.

Mama put on a freshly starched house dress and rolled her long brown hair around a long roll of cotton into a circle that framed her face.

"I'll stop at the Settlement House after I give blood," she said when Mari came home. "We're collecting books for the troops in hospitals. I don't have any books in English except for my prayer book, so I'll offer that. It might comfort some poor soldier."

The house was quiet, so Mari settled down to study for her spelling test on Friday. She read for a while afterward and then said her prayers before bedtime, asking for the war to be over soon.

The Package

On Monday, Mari came home from school to see a big box wrapped in brown paper and tied with string in the middle of the kitchen table. In the upper left-hand corner was an APO number. Army Post Office! The box was from Johnny.

"Mama!" She ran out to the back porch where Mama was in the yard, taking laundry off the clothesline. "There's a box from Johnny."

"I know. The postman delivered it a half hour ago."

"Can't we open it?"

"We'll wait until the others get home."

"What do you suppose he sent? The postmark's so blurry I could barely make out the year: nineteen forty-three."

As a strong gust sent Papa's work pants dancing a frantic jitterbug on the clothesline, Mama changed the subject. "The wind is starting to pick up, Mari. Come help me get these clothes down." Across the alley in Edith Fleming's back yard, they saw one of her sheets fly up and wrap itself around a clothes pole. "On second thought, better run over and tell Edith it's going to rain."

It wasn't unusual for Edith to forget about her laundry. In good weather, the Monday wash might hang on the line into Tuesday or even Wednesday. Edith, probably the only woman for miles around who'd ever been to college, had her own priorities.

"Rain? Really?" she said, peering up at the sky. "I'm afraid I wasn't paying attention. I'm reading a new book, *A Tree Grows in Brooklyn*. It's a *New York Times* bestseller, and I can't bear to put it down."

Mari offered to help Edith bring in her clothes; she was bursting to talk about the box. But Edith said she'd forgotten her laundry basket in the basement and told Mari she'd better get home before the rain came. Mari barely made it across the alley and up the steps before the first few drops began to fall.

"Oh, not Velveeta again!" she groaned as Mama pulled the familiar box out of the refrigerator, the noodles already bubbling on the stove.

123

"You told me you like macaroni and cheese."

"It's all we ever have."

Mama handed her a capsule and a pin. "There's oleo over there on the counter. It's been out long enough to have softened. I'd like to add it to the mac and cheese."

Mari unwrapped the shortening brick and dumped it into a bowl. "Yuk! It looks like lard." She pricked the capsule and squeezed out the yellow dye, watching it make bright orange puddles on the white surface of the shortening. As she stirred, the orange muted into yellow and turned the shortening to what looked like butter. Mama, slicing Velveeta into hot noodles, added the oleo, and then covered the pan. She set out a jar of beets she'd put up last month and poured a can of green beans into a smaller pan while Mari set to slicing the last of the homemade bread.

"Why don't we ever have butter anymore?"

"Butter is scarce. What there is goes to the troops overseas, to men like Johnny."

So many things were scarce. Mama was drinking Postum, but Mari could tell how much she missed her coffee. Postum, powdered grains boiled in water, smelled bad and tasted worse, and Mama finally admitted it did take some getting used to.

Mari sat down at the kitchen table to do her homework, but she couldn't help running her hand over the box, trying to picture where Johnny was when he'd sent it. But mostly, she thought about what could be inside.

Last year, he had sent a box addressed only to Mari. Inside was a Dutch girl's cap and a pair of wooden shoes. Mama found some material in a trunk in the attic and made her a blue cotton dress and a white apron. With her long hair in braids, she came home from the Halloween party at school, brandishing the prize for best costume. The shoes hurt her feet, but the prize, a yellow pencil box covered with pictures of warplanes, was worth it. She kept it in her desk to remind her of Johnny.

"I'm home!" The screen door slammed, and Helen, barely inside, was pulling off her factory Oxfords. "The rain has

124

passed already. Oh, and Mari, I just saw Edith setting out an old cast iron skillet next to her garbage can. You'd better get it before Ronnie picks it up for the scrap drive."

Mari raced out the back door. Lately, that weasel Ronnie Churlin had been trying to knock her out of the running for the Beveridge School scrap champ. Well, she'd show him. Good old Edith. She'd be sure to thank her tomorrow. She spied Papa on his way home from the steel mill, taking a shortcut through the alley. "Hurry, Papa. There's a surprise!" Mari dragged him into the kitchen with his lunch pail still in his hand.

"How did he manage to send such a big box with all the fighting going on over there?" he wondered aloud.

"MaryAnn!" Mari called to her big sister, who was just arriving home from work. "In here! There's a big present for the family."

"Or maybe small presents packed into one big box," MaryAnn said as she kicked off her high heels and dropped into a chair.

"Then there might be perfume!" Helen crooned. "Maybe even French perfume. Is he in France, do you think?"

"How should I know? How can we know anything?"

"We know he's alive," Mama murmured.

"At least he was when he sent it," Helen said softly, turning her head so Mama wouldn't hear.

"Ooh, maybe he sent silk stockings! Tillie at the factory got stockings from her boyfriend. From Italy, she thinks. She said our soldiers can buy stockings on the Black Market really cheap there."

Silk stockings weren't always such a great luxury. They were manufactured right here at Bear Brand Hosiery; that is, until the war, when great quantities of silk were needed for parachutes. So, Helen and the other women stitched parachutes all day long at the factory while MaryAnn slid bare feet into her high heels six mornings a week and covered her bare legs with pancake makeup before she left for work. Mari's job was to draw a black eyebrow pencil line up the back of each leg for instant "stockings." Then MaryAnn trotted to the streetcar line, heading to work to stand from nine to five behind the cosmetics counter at Sears with a half hour for lunch.

They hurried through supper and moved the box back onto the table.

Mama cut the string with her sewing scissors and tore away the paper.

A black lump lay burrowed in a pile of paper. "What is it?"

"A turtle shell?"

"It's a helmet." Papa lifted the scarred metal headgear out of the box and turned it around. "A very old helmet. Must have seen quite a few battles in its time."

"Ugh. What's that silver thing on top?"

"Maybe some sort of decoration?"

"Well, it's an ugly decoration," MaryAnn said, gazing at a silver bulb that tapered up into a sharp spike.

"There's something else." Papa dug under the papers to find a sword wedged crosswise at the bottom of the box. The silver work on the handle matched the silver on the helmet. "It's heavy," he said, using both hands to lift it.

Mari felt chills down her spine as he slid the long knife out of its sheath. The blade looked hostile and deadly. A scrap of paper was crumpled in the corner. "A Prussian officer's helmet and sword."

"Prussians are Germany's elite troops," Papa was telling them, turning the helmet round in his hands. "They are ruthless fighters and feared throughout Europe. When Johnny comes home ..." Papa's voice cracked, and Mari knew he wished his son were there now, "he'll tell us where he got these things. They're very old."

"So much for perfume," Helen sighed.

"Or stockings."

"Why did he send us these things?" MaryAnn rolled her shoulders to ease the tension in her back. "Turn on the radio, Helen. See if you can find some music. I'm sick to death of this war."

They were all sick of it. War was everywhere; it filled the radio, the newspapers, and newsreels at the movie theater

126

uptown. Last week's reel showed British families fleeing to underground shelters while German bombers thundered overhead. Willie Churlin said the Germans might bomb the Gary steel mills if the war didn't end soon. Mari didn't like going to Churlin's Grocery anymore.

Things were so much better before the war. Pearl Harbor had changed them. What seemed important two years ago didn't matter anymore. And not just things like rationing. Now, there were twice-weekly air raid drills. When the siren sounded, they drew heavy curtains across the windows so that no light shone through. A rap on the door meant the warden patrolling the neighborhood had seen a sliver of light somewhere. Mari's school had a surprise air raid drill last Tuesday. Now, she read her Nancy Drew book at night to keep her mind off the war.

"The Prussians invaded my country," Mama was saying. "The Prussians defeated Austria."

Mari perked up. Was Mama talking about the old country?

"Back then, it wasn't called Austria. It was called the Austro-Hungarian Empire. And we didn't have a president like Mr. Roosevelt. We had an emperor; his name was Franz Josef."

"Really? You had an emperor? You mean like a king, right."

"Yes. I saw him once when he rode through our village in a fancy carriage. He wore a white uniform with a bright red sash. I remember ladies tossing flowers and men waving their caps as he passed.

"So, the people liked him? He was a good king?"

"My parents thought so. In Europe, a king decides the religion for his country. His subjects go to the same church he does. If the next king has a different religion, the people change to that religion, too. But when Franz Josef came to power, he said people could worship the same way they always had."

"My papa was the mayor of Vilka—our village," Mama continued. "When there was a dispute, the parties came to our

127

house for Papa to mediate. He had this way of calming everyone down."

"What does he look like?" Mari moved closer.

"He's very tall with red hair. He loves to ride horses. He has a big mustache that tickled when he kissed me goodnight." Mari couldn't be sure, but she thought she actually heard Mama giggle.

Watching her there, smoothing out the brown paper on the table, Mari felt sad. "Did you ever go back to see your parents?"

"No. With six children to raise, there was never enough money. We saved for years, thinking we would bring them here, but it was not to be."

"Why not?"

"Because one day, all the banks in America closed. Overnight, every penny we had saved was gone."

"Who took it? Can't you go to the bank and get it back?"

"No. People all over America lost their savings the same as we did. It was called the Great Depression."

"So now, I'll never see my grandma and grandpa?"

"Maybe after the war. I hope after the war."

Mama had always shushed Mari when she tried to ask about life in the old country. Papa said it was because she hadn't heard from her parents for a long time. Mari knew her friend Sylvia was anxious about her parents too, just like Mama.

"Our emperor Franz Josef died after I came to America. Now, thirty years later, the Nazis march across Europe, conquering one country after another. The whole world has changed."

"Why do they do that?"

"Because Adolph Hitler loves power," Papa said. "He is the Nazi leader. He calls Germans 'The Master Race.'"

"So, people in the countries they invade are like their slaves? Anybody who isn't German has to be a slave?"

"In his mind, yes."

"I wouldn't want to be a slave."

"That's why our soldiers, like Johnny and Peter, have gone there, to free the people."

"Why is Hitler so mean? Didn't his mother take him to Sunday School?"

"I don't know. Maybe not."

"I can still see the guards that followed Franz Josef's carriage," Mama continued with a faraway look. "They rode fine horses and had long swords, but their helmets had white plumes, not spikes, on top."

That evening, Papa found an old belt and hitched it through the slits below the sword handle so Mari could hang the sword at her side. It was too long, but if she pushed down, she could tilt the blade and keep it from scraping the floor. She paraded up and down the front room, pretending to be one of Franz Josef's guards.

The next day, Mari hurried home from school to put on the helmet, hang the sword at her side, and march around the front yard. First, she pretended to fight Germans, but the sword was heavy, and her arm grew tired, so she went back to marching, feeling very important in her gear.

"Hey, Mari! What are you doing?"

Lon, the boy from her class, was leaning over the fence, watching her. She hadn't seen him come up.

"I'm just marching. Can't you see?"

"Where'd you get that Kraut stuff?"

"My brother Johnny sent it."

"No kidding? The guy that's in the army? He sent you that stuff?" Lon's little piggy eyes drilled into her like black bullets.

"Hey, Donald, get a load of this," Lon said to his friend who had come up beside him. "Mari's brother killed a kraut."

"He did not. He just ..."

"Aw, come on Mari. He killed a German and sent you the proof."

Mari's face flamed. Johnny wasn't a killer.

"So, you're not a Kraut lover after all," Lon scoffed, and Donald laughed.

Mari snatched the helmet from her head and turned toward the house. It was never any use talking to those two, anyway.

Mama was gone, but she found Papa in his tool shed out back and asked him, "Did Johnny kill this man and send us his things?"

She felt sure Papa would give a good reason for the things that had come in the box. Instead, he looked at her for a long time.

"I don't know," he said finally. "It's war." His eyes dimmed and he turned back to his worktable.

Mari was scared sometimes by blackouts and air raid drills at school. Now she looked down at the helmet, felt the weight of the deadly sword at her side, and shivered. Suddenly, she was very afraid—not for herself, but for Johnny.

Weeks passed by, and then months. A long, cold winter finally rolled into spring. Mari missed her brother terribly. She and Mama wrote letters and baked pastries, packing them carefully into boxes to send. Yet, in wartime, there was no guarantee the packages would ever reach her brother at all. A letter from Johnny always brought tears to Mama's eyes. Mari knew it was because that letter meant that for the time being, at least, her son was alive.

One day, Mari came home from school to smell something wonderful the minute she stepped in the door. Apple pie.

Johnny Comes Home on Leave

"Hey, Bamboozle—remember me?"

Mari couldn't believe her ears. Her brother's arms lifted her from behind and whirled her around the room. When Johnny set her down, Mari turned to face the tanned stranger in the army uniform. She saw the Lightning Division patch on his cap, the Ranger insignia on his shoulder, and the sparkle in her brother's bright blue eyes. She hugged him then, laughing as she breathed in the strong medicine smell of Lifebuoy soap. When Mama came into the room wiping her hands on her apron, they caught her up, as well, and the three of them danced together around the room.

Papa came home from work, followed by MaryAnn and Helen. They all agreed Mama had used most of the month's rationing coupons on that one meal, but it was worth it. Round steak fried with onions, mashed potatoes, *kapusta* (Austrian-style cabbage), green beans, and homemade rolls and butter. And for dessert, apple pie. Johnny always said Mama could make a pie worth fighting for. No puny little pies in their house, but an enormous, golden-brown pie that filled out a cookie sheet size pan. *It was a meal,* Mari thought, *as wonderful as the moment.*

After supper, the girls washed the dishes, then everyone went out on the front porch to enjoy the fresh spring air. Mari ran to get the Prussian helmet and strapped the sword to her side. She marched up and down the length of the porch, showing off for her brother.

"Where did you get them, John?" Papa asked, pointing to the gear.

Johnny crossed his legs and looked up at the big oak tree in the front yard. That tree had shaded their front porch as long as Mari could remember. "From a battle in a German forest. They belonged to a German officer. He died."

Mari saw her father turn to look more closely at his son. Johnny gazed westward where the setting sun, like a flaming beach ball, hung low in the afternoon sky.

"He must have come from a long line of officers, Pop. He wore that helmet and the sword right on the battlefield."

Carrying a tray with glasses and a pitcher of lemonade, MaryAnn came back onto the porch. She set the tray down and began to pour drinks, careful not to look at her brother when she spoke. "Did you kill him, John?"

Mari watched her brother's mouth tighten. He didn't look at his sister, either, but just kept looking at the sky as he answered. "The fighting was very bad that day. We kept on moving closer and closer to the German lines. Finally, we broke through."

"You shoot him?" Papa asked.

Mari saw Mama send a warning look in Papa's direction. "There are *rozki* in the cookie jar, Mari. Put them on a plate and bring them out here." She started to shake her head, but when she saw the look on Mama's face, she could tell there was no room for argument. So, Mari went inside. But instead of going into the kitchen, she stayed out of sight near the open screen door, listening. Everyone's eyes were riveted on her brother.

"Hand-to-hand combat, Pop. We fought the Germans one at a time and we took them out one by one." Johnny shrugged. "Or the other way around."

"How?" MaryAnn wanted to know.

"Bayonets." Johnny looked down at his hands. "Or whatever it took."

MaryAnn put down the glass she was holding and walked to the other end of the porch. Mari could see her lean over the railing and pull an oak leaf from the tree. Resting both elbows on the rail, her sister stood for a long time, rubbing the leaf between her fingers. "You killed him, and then you sent us his helmet and sword? Why?" When her brother didn't say anything, MaryAnn turned to him. "I never believed you could kill anyone, John."

When Johnny spoke, his voice was so low Mari had to strain to hear. "I never believed it, either. But I saw my men falling on either side of me. I heard them screaming. I watched them die." She saw her brother's jaw working.

"Why did you send us his things?"

Her brother looked at MaryAnn, who was now living back at her parents' house, with eyes that were hard and bright. "I sent them because he was a lousy Kraut who was killing my men and was ready to kill me, that's why. I sent them because he was a Prussian, and Mom and Pop talked all those years about the mighty invincible Prussians. The mighty Prussians." Mari could see the veins pulsing in her brother's neck. His voice was loud. "I sent them because that day we, by God, beat their Prussian asses!"

Johnny's shoulders sagged. He looked weary. Mari could see the lines in his face. She hadn't ever noticed those lines before. But she saw them clearly now, the deep furrows carved razor sharp into his skin. Johnny looked at MaryAnn and his eyes softened. "I know that Kraut didn't have any more choice than I did about being on that battlefield. Funny, I can still see him, how surprised he looked when I ...."

Johnny was looking at his family, but Mari could tell he wasn't seeing them at all.

"He was young, you know. About twenty, maybe. Blonde. In some other place, we might have been friends. But there, in those woods, he was my enemy. And he died doing what he had to do. He died fighting for his country like I was fighting for mine."

The sun quickly sank below the horizon, and a gray dusk settled over the porch. Mari felt as though some thick, pale blanket had been thrown over her family, keeping them from the light. She heard Mama's soft accent, "I wonder, did the German have family ... or a girlfriend?" Her mother's voice grew thin. "I wonder how his parents heard about him." Mama's words trailed off, and the only sound was the breeze rustling the leaves of the big oak tree.

Mari looked down at the sword still hanging at her side. Unbuckling her belt, she took off first the sword and then the helmet. Her head felt clammy and her hair damp, like she had just stepped out of the shower. Sadness hung like dead weight from her heart. Mari went upstairs into her bedroom and took a chair from the corner. Walking to the other side of the room, she opened the closet door and climbed up onto the chair. Standing on tiptoe, she laid the helmet and the sword on the very top shelf. Then she climbed down and closed the door again. War, she thought, was a terrible and confusing time.

But one thing was very clear. Mari didn't want to play soldier anymore. Not ever again.

Where The Heroes Are

"Where are all your medals, John?" Mama said as she looked up from braiding Mari's hair the next morning.

Johnny, tall and trim in his infantry uniform with the Ranger insignia on the shoulder, tapped nervous fingers on his pant legs.

"I don't wear medals, Mom." He was looking through the front room window at the porch shaded from the afternoon sun by the big oak tree in the yard.

"You should wear your decorations, John. You should be proud."

Johnny had been twice wounded in action. Yesterday, he'd surprised Mari when she came home from school, jumping out from behind the kitchen door, and scooping her up to twirl her around the room, just like the old days. But when he put her down, he kept looking at her, telling Mama over and over how much she'd grown. Well, she was in the fifth grade, after all. Still, she hoped being bigger was all right. She wanted everything to be just the way it was before he went away to fight. Nothing could ruin these next two weeks with Johnny. Nothing.

He her a playful punch on the arm. "Well, Bamboozle, ready to go? We don't want to keep my old buddy waiting."

Mari loved it when he called her Bamboozle. It let her know things were just like they were before he left. She was pleased that Johnny had invited her to come along with him to visit his friend Mike. Johnny had always let her tag along.

"Put on your medals, John. I want people to know you're a hero."

"Don't call me that!"

Mari sucked in her breath and watched him stalk out of the room.

"He fights for his country. He should wear the medals."

Mari didn't know what to say. Johnny never talked to Mama like that. And everything had been so good until now. Maybe Mama thought the medals could make up for the worry lines around her mouth. Maybe they were salve for the telegram the Army sent two months ago, "We regret to inform you that Staff Sergeant John Cmar has been reported missing in action." But months later he had reappeared, and the worry was put back in the box. Mama looked lost. She went over to the credenza and stood for a long time looking at the family pictures lined up across the top—Peter Jr. in his flight uniform, and MaryAnn with Rick in the Colorado mountains.

"Are we ready to roll, Midget?"

Johnny was back and he had a double row of medals on his chest. He looked uncomfortable, but Mari knew how much he loved Mama and was trying to please her. She pointed to the brightest medal. "What's that one?"

"The Silver Star."

Mari remembered the *Stars and Stripes* article an army buddy had sent them. She could almost recite the words by heart, "Pinned down by heavy enemy fire, Sgt. John Cmar single-handedly held off the Germans for two days when everyone else in his unit had been killed." It even had his picture, hand-drawn and probably copied from some old photograph. Then Mari pointed to a square metal cross hung from a multicolored ribbon.

"What's that?"

"Croix de Guerre," he said. "It means war cross. It's given by the French government."

"Why did they give you a medal?"

"Well," he said sitting on the arm of the sofa, "Intelligence dropped me behind enemy lines, and I fought with the French Freedom Fighters. Some of the bravest men I've ever met."

Mama came to sit beside him on the sofa. "Is that when the Army sent word that you were missing?"

"They told you that?"

"Yes," she said. "But they never said you had been wounded.

Johnny put his arm around his mother's shoulder. She was trying to hold back the tears. "Hey, Mom. It's okay."

Mari wanted to know about the colored bars above the medals.

"Campaign ribbons," he said. "Places where the battles were." Johnny looked at his watch and gave his mother's shoulder a pat before getting to his feet. He picked up his cap. "We're late, Squirt. Time to go."

Mari didn't want to leave. She wanted to hear about the other medals, but later, walking the six blocks to his friend's house, Johnny let Mari wear his cap. In a short time, they reached Mike's house.

"So, John, how's it going?"

Mike Kaylas was pumping Johnny's hand and pounding him on the back as he hurried them both into the house. Even Mrs. Kaylas came in from the kitchen, tucking wisps of hair behind one ear and then wiping her hands on a dishtowel. She shook John's hand, telling him how handsome he looked in his uniform. Mari looked around the room at the dark blue sofa and matching chairs with white crocheted doilies pinned to their headrests. The coarse covering on the sofa pricked her bare legs when she sat.

Mari listened as the two men talked about friends and families. Mike and his mother said how much the neighborhood had changed, what with the war and all. Mari shifted. The prickly sofa was making the skin on her legs numb.

"George Yaros was home a few months ago," Mike said. "Just got out of basic. Not sure where he's headed next. He says the army won't say. Military secret."

Mari thought of the letters Johnny had sent from the front, letters with entire lines covered over by a thick black marker. Those must have been secrets, too.

Mike lit a Lucky Strike and blew smoke in a big white puff out of his nose. He leaned in close to her brother. "So, how was it over there? Pretty rough?"

"Yeah. Pretty rough."

Mike crushed out his cigarette in the glass ashtray and leaned back on the sofa.

"You know we're doing our part here too, John. I work double shifts a lot at the mill because you guys need the steel."

"I know, Mike. We couldn't do it without you fellas back here."

"I tried to enlist, you know. They wouldn't take me. Flat feet."

Johnny crossed one leg over the other.

"You kill a lot of Germans?"

Johnny's mouth settled in a thin, straight line. He looked away.

"That how you got all those medals, John? What did they give you the medals for?"

"Good conduct, mostly," Johnny grinned.

Mike threw back his head and laughed but wouldn't let it go. "Tell us how many Germans you killed, man. How does it feel to be a hero?"

"Don't ever call me that!"

Mari saw two red streaks climbing up Johnny's neck. His loud voice startled her. Mike and his mother stared in surprise as Johnny got to his feet.

"You want to see a hero, Mike? Look at the wooden boxes they carry off military planes! Go see the rows of white markers at Arlington Cemetery. *Those* are the heroes. Don't ever forget that! Find yourself a cemetery, Mike. That's where the heroes are!"

They quickly took their leave and were suddenly back out on the sidewalk. Neither of them said anything as they walked home. On the way, Johnny stopped in front of Whitey's Tavern.

"I'm going in here, Mari. You go home. Tell Mama I'll be back in a little while."

Mari watched him go inside the bar. She badly wanted to follow him and beg him to come home, but she knew children weren't allowed in there. She turned the corner and kept walking down the tree-lined street. Leaves rustled softly in the breeze, shimmering silver-green in the sunlight. Flowers brightened the front yards of neatly painted houses.

Then she looked up and saw it again, the gold star hanging in Mrs. Trudis's window. On school days, Mari always looked straight ahead when she passed the Trudis's House. When she forgot, she felt the same painful jab in her stomach that she did now. Mrs. Trudis would never see her boy again. And Johnny—he'd be going back to the front before long. She could taste the fear in her mouth.

She told her friend Sylvia she couldn't play that afternoon because her brother was home on leave. She helped Mama make a special dinner with all his favorite foods. With the rest of the rationing coupons, there was butter for the homemade biscuits, and Mama had hoarded enough sugar for another pie. But when dinner was ready, Johnny hadn't returned. They waited for a long time until, finally, everything got cold. They put all the food back in the ice box.

Later that night, Mari had a stomachache and had to take some Pepto Bismol and lie down. She was reading her Nancy Drew book when she heard Johnny's voice. Coming into the bedroom, he put his hand on her forehead and said she felt warm. But Mari felt better already having him sit beside her on the bed.

"Want to sing some songs?"

She rose up on one elbow. They always sang together. It started on the Ferris wheel at carnival time back before the war. She was a little kid and afraid of riding up so high, but Johnny had put his arm around her. He told her they'd sing and everything would be all right.

"Life's evening sun
Is sinking low
A few more days
And I must go
To meet the deed
That I have done
Where there will be
No setting sun."

He sang again, and then they sang together. Johnny asked if she wanted to hear any more songs. He tapped his foot and went on. "Oomp tee, oomp tee, oom pah pa. You know, like first you go pee-pee and then you go … poopy."

When he laughed, his breath smelled like vinegar. He smelled like used smoke when he kissed her goodnight. He stood up, swaying slightly, and was lurching sideways on his way out of her room.

Later that night, Mari dreamed she was all alone on the Ferris wheel; it started spinning faster and faster. She woke to find her nightgown soaked through. Mama's worried face raced through her mind. She dozed again and was standing in a long aisle with white crosses on either side. They were so close she could touch them. She began running hard to get away from that terrible place. Finally out of breath, she stopped short, gasping for air. Something shiny caught her eye. She stooped to pick it up but froze. It was a gold star.

Mari pulled the covers up tight around her, then buried her face in the pillow so no one could hear her cry.

The Mump

"My head hurts, Mrs. Martin. And I'm cold."

"Your forehead does feel warm," Mrs. Martin said with her hand on Mari's brow. "And I can see that you're shaky. Better head over to Miss Hendersen's office. You may need to lie down."

Within the hour, Mama appeared in the nurse's office to walk Mari home.

Dr. Wimmer came by later that evening.

"It's the mumps, all right," he said, gently probing Mari's jaws as she sat up in bed. "No school for you, young lady. At least for the rest of the week."

One side of Mari's jaw hurt when she touched it, but she told him the other side felt fine.

"You'll hurt on the other side, too," he promised. But she never did. In the mirror, she looked lopsided, like there was a rubber ball stuck in one of her cheeks.

After a week of rest and chicken soup, and later mashed potatoes and Jello, Mari perked up and begged to go to the library with Sylvia.

"I had a mump," she told Sylvia as they headed uptown that afternoon.

"You had the mumps?"

"No. Just one. I had a mump." She liked saying it, feeling special and silly at the same time.

"Let's walk this way today," Sylvia said.

They passed a yarn shop and one that sold second-hand clothes.

"Phew! It smells musty," Sylvia said when an old man came out carrying a wrinkled brown bag. The tiny store next door had comic books and postcards.

"When he came to America, Papa learned English by hanging around shops like these," Mari told Sylvia. "He sounded out the words on postcards until he could read them all. And he started reading the newspaper front to back, even the death notices and the society page. Now, he helps men and women with English if they want a job at the steel mill."

"Look, Mari! A new *Wonder Woman* comic book! Do you have a dime?"

But Mari wasn't listening. Instead, she grabbed Sylvia's arm and dragged her next door to A-1 Pawn.

"Look! There in the window."

"What"

"The Nazi helmet. The sword."

"Are they yours?"

"No. Mine are in the closet. Let's go inside."

"Why?"

"To see what they cost. To see who will pay for creepy stuff like this."

It was a dark hallway of a store jammed with all kinds of things: high-top gym shoes that looked brand new, a pearly white accordion in an open case, an old toaster, a green-speckled bowling ball with size ten bowling shoes, an old Victrola with a crank on one side.

Two men were at the counter. The older, dark-haired one, ramrod straight, kept jabbing, "Is a good watch. Worth much money. You give us good price."

"Well, now, I can't make out this writing on the back, Mister. And I never
heard of this watchmaker."

"Is good company. Very good watchmaker. Worth much money."

"I'm not sure," the clerk said, turning the watch over again.

The nervous blond man beside him kept looking around, tugging at coat sleeves that kept riding up over his bony wrists.

"His clothes are too small," Sylvia whispered.

Seeing Sylvia watching him, he leaned into the older man and whispered something in his ear. Without a word, they took the watch and hurried out of the shop.

"Odd pair," the clerk said as they watched them move up the street. "I heard that man talking German, Mari," Sylvia said in a low voice.

"Lots of people talk German, Sylvia."

"You girls buyin' or sellin'?" The clerk chuckled at his own joke.

"How much for the helmet and sword?" Mari asked.

"Three-fifty. Real collector's items. You girls got any money?"

"Tell him about the German man, Mari!" Sylvia whispered.

Just then, a woman came in dragging a small boy by the hand. "Don't touch anything, Joey. Be a good boy, and I'll buy you a sucker when we're done. That toaster work?" she asked the clerk.

"Like a charm! I'll plug it in so you can see how nice she heats up." He took the toaster from the shelf and set it on the counter.

"Thank you for your time," Mari said in her most polite voice. They hurried into the street, craning their necks for any sight of the pair, but the men were gone. The girls kept a lookout for several blocks and then doubled back, but they were nowhere to be seen.

"We should have said something, Mari."

"Said what? A man was speaking German in your store?"

"Did you notice the younger one? He was really nervous."

"Anyway, they're both gone now. We'll stay on guard, just in case."

"I just know there was something funny going on there."

"Oh my gosh, Sylvia! I told Mama we'd be back by four." The big clock on the bank across the street showed four-fifteen, so they turned toward home.

"And we never made it to the library, either."

The Dime Store

Even before she rolled over and opened her eyes, Mari knew that Mama was brewing Postum again. The house smelled like boiled rags.

"I gave the last cup of coffee to Papa before he left for work; he looked so worn out." Papa was working longer shifts, seven days a week, and they could see the strain around his eyes. Mama had worry lines to match. "What I miss most in this war is a good cup of coffee, and I don't know how long this rationing will last." She took a whiff of the liquid in her cup, made a face, and set it back down again.

"I thought we were going Christmas shopping," Mari said, changing the subject to cheer her up.

"We are," she replied and actually smiled. "And what would you say to lunch at Woolworth's Dime Store?"

"I'd say *yes!*"

It had turned colder overnight, so they burrowed into their coats as they tramped along the icy sidewalk to the streetcar line. The streetcar was crowded with ladies hoping to fill their big cloth bags with Christmas presents when they reached uptown. It was standing room only, but the mood was merry since December 25th was only a week away.

The car stopped a block from Woolworth's, and Mari watched her breath come out in little puffs when they stepped into the street and hurried to the store. When she opened the door, the warm air greeted them like a welcome blanket, and Mari unbuttoned her coat.

"I smell popcorn, Mama! Can we get some?"

"The nickel bag. And don't gulp, or you'll get a stomachache."

"Nothing beats popcorn at Woolworth's!"

In the sheet music section, a skinny, dark-haired girl played Christmas music on the Victrola, and "Jingle Bells" tinkled in the air. War or no war, Mari was sure that her heart was going to burst with joy. Christmas just did that to you.

She polished off her popcorn, checked her pocket to make sure the allowance money she'd been saving was still there,

144

and headed to pick out Papa's present. She settled on a pair of linen handkerchiefs with his initials in the corner. Then Mama knew to go to another part of the store while Mari looked for her present. She found beads, sky blue like Mama's eyes. Last Christmas, MaryAnn helped Mari shop, but now she was old enough to do it on her own.

"These are lovely," the pretty young clerk said. "They must be for someone very special."

"My mama."

"I'm sure she'll love them."

"Our Christmas is on January seventh," Mari explained. "But we wanted to shop this week before everything gets picked over."

"I've never heard of Christmas on January seventh."

A clerk came over from the next counter. "My grandparents on my father's side have Christmas on that day, too. They call it Russian Christmas."

"We're not Russian," Mari said.

"Even if they're not Russian, many Eastern Europeans celebrate on that day," the clerk told the other girl.

"How do you like having Christmas a week later?"

"I like it. We don't have to go to school if the seventh lands on a school day."

Mama had been saving for months for a sheepskin jacket for Papa, so they headed next to Goldblatt's Department Store.

"Not the basement, Mari. Not today."

Clothes in the basement were cheaper. Many were "seconds," clothes with crooked seams, uneven stitches, or other flaws. A flaw meant the item was marked down. But even if you looked carefully, the defect could be hard to find and you could come home with a bargain. On the main floor, they found a heavy coat with a sheepskin lining.

"Now Papa will have a warm coat to get him through the winter. He roams all over the mill fixing machines, and I know he gets cold." Satisfied, Mama put the bulky coat in her big shopping bag.

"Why doesn't Papa buy presents?"

"The stores are closed by the time he gets off work. Besides, his paycheck is our present all year long."

The lunch counter in the basement was always crowded, and today was the busiest Mari had ever seen it. They finally snagged two seats together, and Mama ordered the vegetable plate like she always did, and Mari had a toasted cheese sandwich and a cherry Coke. They caught the four o'clock streetcar home.

Papa was working late again, so he missed the evening news.

"Good evening, Mr. and Mrs. America and all the ships at sea. Flash! We have late word from the Russian Front." Walter Winchel's staccato voice punched out the story over the rat-tat-tat telegraph machine pulsing in the background.

"This month, December nineteen forty-two, with the temperature at forty-five degrees below zero and the Germans only twelve miles from Moscow, Soviet troops are starting to push the Germans back where they came from."

"Dear God, I'm so grateful for any bit of good news," Mama sighed. "But it won't seem like Christmas without Johnny."

"I'm going to find us a tree, Mama. I'll find one just like he used to."

"There's no need, Mari. For the past few years, we couldn't afford a Christmas tree because of the Depression, so Johnny went through the alleys to find one that someone had thrown away. But with Papa working so much overtime this year, we can buy our own."

"I'll find one that's bigger and prettier than any tree we can afford. He told me rich families throw out perfectly good trees right after Christmas."

"We'll buy one," she said again, and Mari knew an order when she heard one.

"The lot closed last week," said a burly man who saw them looking at the empty corner the next day. "We only had a few trees to begin with; they're scarce this year. With all the men gone, there's nobody left to cut them down. People are buying artificial. It's the new thing. But if you ask me, the fake ones look about as nice as those branches on the ground." They looked over at the few scraggly branches scattered in the dirt.

"Don't worry, we'll have a tree—a real one, too. Sylvia said she'd help me find one. Papa can carry it home after work."

But Papa said no. He was too tired to haul some family's leftover Christmas tree across town. They should get a fake fir from the hardware store; there were sure to be markdowns the day after Christmas.

The next night, December 24th, they sat in the front room and listened to President Roosevelt speak to the nation. "It is a happier Christmas Eve than last year," he said, "because the forces of darkness are less confident of success in their evil ways."

"I don't feel happier," Mari said. "I feel sad. I wish Johnny was home. Peter and Rick, too."

"Tomorrow, Christmas day," the President went on, "I have ordered all defense plants shut down. It will be the only holiday this year. Christmas is a holy day, so may all it stands for live and grow throughout the years." To the troops, he added, "Christmas prayers follow you wherever you may be."

Mari looked over to see tears on Mama's cheeks. When the President signed off, everyone was quiet for a long time.

They all went to church the next day, and afterward, Papa slept through most of his day off. On Saturday, he went back to work, and Mari went with Mama to the hardware store. It was their one day to get a tree because all the stores were closed on Sundays.

"Sorry. We sold all our trees before Christmas," the clerk said. "Matter of fact, we sold them all the same day they came in."

They tried everywhere, but it was the same story. Hungry and discouraged, they came back home. Later, Mama sent Mari to Churlin's for some beans and potatoes for supper.

"Alvin Smiley thought he spotted the German prisoners in the alley behind his garage. He called the cops, but by the time they got there, they were gone," said Willie Churlin as he scurried around filling an order for old Mrs. Krason, who lived

147

down the block. "Just between us," he leaned over the counter and lowered his voice, "Ed Pulver, the police sergeant, told me they almost nabbed the pair last week." Willie looked over at Mari and put his finger up to his lips. "Loose lips sink ships, Mari." Mari didn't have any information that would sink ships, but she nodded like she knew what Willie was talking about.

At school, the kids jabbered about what they got for Christmas. Sylvia was quiet because she celebrated a holiday called Hanukkah, and Mari was waiting for January 7th.

Each day, Mari checked the alley. No tree.

Early Thursday morning, she heard Papa banging around in the basement, shoveling coal into the furnace. She lay in bed a little longer until the radiator in her room clunked, the signal that it was starting to warm up.

Tonight was Russian Christmas Eve, and she was off school because of the big teachers' conference. She should have been happy, but Mari didn't feel much like Christmas. What was Christmas without a tree? Mama was trying to make a holiday dinner, but Kresny already sold all the meat to the "Americans" who had their Christmas on December 25th. No, he couldn't get ham, couldn't get anything at all but "Victory Sausages," plain old hot dogs. Worst of all, they hadn't heard from Johnny, not for a long time. All morning, Mari helped Mama cook and clean until the house was spotless.

One bright spot was homemade bread. Three big loaves were shining golden brown on top of the stove. And Sylvia came over that afternoon.

"Where should we go?" Sylvia asked.

"Have to go across town. I've looked everywhere around here."

Before they set out, they hooked pinkies. "Last chance, do or die, Custer's last stand. Don't forget the sled, Mari."

"Mama! It's snowing," Mari called as they headed out. The ground was already covered in white, and it was still snowing in big fluffy flakes that landed soft and wet when you stuck out your tongue. There were footprints on the snow-covered sidewalk but none in the alley. Very few people were out.

They crossed the street and headed for the alleys where the really rich people lived. All afternoon, they tramped from one block to another. One sad tree with the needles mostly gone was tilted against a fence.

"It's getting late, Mari. We should quit."

"One more block, Sylvia. Please." They trudged to almost the end of the last block. "There, Sylvia!" Leaning against a back fence was a huge fir tree. "Holy smoke, it's so tall!"

"It's beautiful! Perfect. Like a picture."

"There's still tinsel left on the branches."

"But it's so big. How can we get it to your house?"

"We'll tip it over so we can pull it."

Toppling the tree was harder than they bargained for. Mari reached into the center to grab the trunk, but the needles raked her face and dug into her knit cap.

"I'll do it. I'm taller." Sylvia grabbed the trunk higher up and managed to push it to the ground. It fell with a heavy thud. They tried to pull it, but it wouldn't budge

"Here now! What are you girls up to?"

A stern-faced woman had opened the back door of the house and was glaring at them.

"Oh, Mari. She thinks we're stealing her tree!"

"I'm sorry, Ma'am. We thought it was all right to take the tree since it was next to the trash barrel."

Pulling on her coat as the door slammed behind her, the woman charged across the yard.

"What mischief are you up to? Christmas is over. What do you want with my tree?"

"It's the only one we could find. It's for Russian Christmas."

"What is Russian Christmas?"

"It's Christmas on January seventh. Tonight is our Christmas Eve. Mama and I tried to buy a tree, but they were sold out. I didn't think you needed this one anymore."

"You say you tried to buy a tree?"

"At the fresh lot across town and then at the hardware store. We tried all over town."

"And how do you plan to move it?" she asked stonily.

149

"I'm not sure. We can't lift it, and Papa is too tired to help us."

"And just why is he so tired?" she asked in an icy tone.

"He's working extra hours at the mill because it's wartime."

The lady paused, and her face softened. "You girls wait right here." She went over to the garage. "Noah! Noah, come out here!"

A tall man in a red plaid jacket came out; he wore a fur cap with the ear flaps hanging down, and he was young. Mari wondered why he wasn't in the army until she saw how he dragged one leg as he came toward them.

"These girls need to get this tree home. It's much too big. See if you can cut some off the bottom so they can cart it home," and she went back in the house without another word.

"You have a beautiful home," Mari said politely as she looked at Noah as he examined the tree.

"Oh, I'm just the handyman," he said. "Mrs. Sturgill must like you girls. She doesn't usually warm up to strangers. There have been vandals lately, so she's skittish. Wartime jitters, I suppose."

Noah cut off over a third of the tree, but it was so big it ended up the perfect size. Then he trimmed the bottom branches to make the trunk fit into a tree stand and even found a rope to tie it to the sled they dragged behind them.

"Merry Christmas," he said, sending them on their way.

On the walk back, it started snowing again. Before Sylvia turned toward home, Mari pulled a ball of string from her pocket.

"Next week, I'll teach you the Jacob's ladder and cat's cradle at recess."

"And I'll tell my grandma how to look for a Christmas tree." Sylvia pocketed the string and headed home.

The Capture

On Christmas night, January 7th, Papa, Mama, and the girls ate by candlelight. A single taper flickered in the center of the kitchen table "to remind us of the star of Bethlehem," Mama said. The lights on the tree in the front room shone through the doorway into the kitchen, too.

"I'm going to write to Johnny about the tree," Mari said.

"You're not eating your soup. Is something wrong?"

"No, Mama. It's good."

She didn't tell her that tonight it tasted different.

She remembered her days mushroom hunting with Johnny in late October. He'd let her tag along as soon as she could hold the pillowcase high enough to keep it from dragging it on the ground. They brought them home to dry so that Mama could make her "famous mushroom soup" for Christmas dinner. Johnny could tell the mushrooms from the poisonous toadstools, but Mama always checked the batch again when they got home, just to make sure.

They would trek through the dark woods where the rich, damp smell of the earth was strong. She loved how the leaves rustled when the wind picked up and listening for the different songs the birds sang. Last year, they even found deer tracks. Being together in the dark, quiet woods was one of her favorite memories of Johnny. This year, she went with Mama.

"I know. I miss Johnny, too." Mama sighed. "So many things have changed."

Even the soup, Mari thought.

"These 'Victory Sausages' taste so good on your Mama's homemade bread." Papa winked. "Let's have them for Christmas dinner from now on." He'd been making jokes about eating hot dogs all evening, trying his best to cheer them up.

"The smell of fresh pine makes the house smell like Christmas," Mama chimed in. "Mari, tomorrow you can take a loaf of bread to the lady who gave us her tree."

"Noah, the handyman, is the one who cut it so I could get it home, and he made it fit in our tree stand."

"Him, too."

The telephone rang, and Mari ran to answer it.

"Wrong number," she said. "There's no one here named Jack."

But Papa hurried over and took the phone. "Okay, Stan. I'll be right there. I'll take the next streetcar."

"Oh, Peter! Not work. Not on Christmas!"

"It's all right. I'll eat when I get home." He kissed Mama's forehead. "Why did the man on the phone call you Jack?" Mari asked when Papa came out of the bedroom, pulling on his sheepskin coat.

Mama answered for him, "Papa's boss calls him 'Jack of All Trades' because he fixes so many machines at the mill."

After Papa slipped out into the night, Mama and the girls finished dinner. They did the dishes and settled in the front room, where the lights on the tree cheered them.

"I'm glad we used different colors," Mari said. "I think all blue lights would make me too sad this year."

They cranked up the Victrola and played some Christmas music, but mostly they just sang carols. Mama sang an old country lullaby and then a funny song about a fancy lady who had lots of boyfriends. She looked so stylish wearing her new beads. They talked about how it would be when the boys came home.

After Mama went to bed, Mari got her coat out of the bedroom. She tiptoed out and huddled in the old rocker on the front porch, looking up at what had to be a million stars in the sky.

Were there stars where Johnny was? He said it was cold there. Did he have a warm coat? Maybe tomorrow there would be a letter. It had been such a long time. She looked over the quiet street, at the dark houses now just dim outlines in the moonlight. But across the alley, the moon splashed bright light on the cement smokehouse, and the hut was almost white in its rays.

Mari leaned forward. A dark shadow was moving along the smokehouse wall. After a while, another shadow inched along behind it. Low voices talked in an urgent whisper. She strained to make out the words. "Nine!" a man's harsh voice spat and then gibberish, words she couldn't understand. He said something about the number nine. Finally, she caught on. Not the number nine, but the *"nein"* that meant "no." They were talking German!

Each shadow carried something, a pile clutched to the chest. Mari sneaked down the porch steps into the front yard. She crouched and moved low along the fence. She could hear grunts like the loads were heavy.

"Dummkopf!" You fool, a voice spat as something tumbled from the taller one's pile. When he bent to pick it up, more pieces fell, and he scrambled to gather everything up again. They muttered and jabbered at each other, then moved around the corner of the smokehouse and out of sight.

Like many families in the neighborhood, Churlin's had a long, narrow city lot. The grocery store was on the corner, facing the opposite street. A small house was attached to the back of the store, a patch of grass behind it. That was the back yard. And behind that, on the alley, was the smokehouse.

Mari sneaked out of her gate, careful to close it quietly, and moved across the alley. Hugging the smokehouse wall, she followed them. The moon went behind a cloud, so she peeked around the corner where they'd gone. She knew the hut door was at the side.

The smokehouse door creaked open, and dim lights went on inside. They had flashlights! They dropped the bundles they carried and pushed the scattered pieces of wood into a pile. One man took off his gloves and stood rubbing his hands together.

"Ist kalt!" he said, searching his pockets.

"Ja. Kalt." Yeah. It's cold.

She heard a scraping sound and saw the flame. They were cold and building a fire! She watched them bend into the flickering tongues on the floor, warming their hands, and almost felt sorry for them. But they were prisoners, German prisoners. She needed to call the police.

EEEEEEE! A sharp cry cut the air!

The light went out and she froze. As the door shut, she slithered back toward the alley. When the door creaked again, one of the men crept out.

AAAyyyOO!

"Vas is dis?" the second one asked, coming up behind.

On the fence, a dark form outlined by moonlight hissed at something she couldn't see. It moved, back hunched, along the top of the fence.

AAAyyyOO!

Then came a guttural laugh behind her and a muttered, *"Katzen!"* Cats! before the Germans melted back into the hut.

Moses, Edith's huge Tabby cat, jumped down from the fence and came to rub against Mari's leg. "Good kitty," she whispered, grateful she wasn't tracking prisoners alone.

Relieved, she'd turned again to go and call the police when the big yellow tomcat from next door jumped onto the fence. The cat was called Caruso, after the famous opera singer, because of the lung volume he could muster. He hissed and hunched, ready for a fight. Moses swung to the fence again, and then Mrs. Trudis's cat showed up, ready for some action, and they all went at it, Caruso in the lead with his paws jabbing and fur flying. It was a noisy battle.

"Caruso! Shut up!" Willie Churlin, who slept with his window ajar all year round, was not in a good mood.

"Willie, come quick!" Mari was at his window.

"Mari, that you? What are you doing out there?"

"It's the Germans, Willie. They're in the smokehouse."

"Our smokehouse?"

"Yes!"

"You sure?"

"Yes. Hurry!"

"It's three a.m.! What are they doing in the smokehouse? Never mind. I'll get my coat!" Willie appeared in his galoshes, his coat buttoned over his nightshirt.

"Go get Mr. Stamkos. I'll keep 'em busy."

Mari flew across the street and roused the Stamkos family. Mr. Stamkos was at work, but little Julie Stamkos ran to their neighbors for help, and Mrs. Stamkos called the police.

The cats were caterwauling, making such a ruckus that the dogs in the neighborhood perked up. Obligated to join in, they started howling and woofing and yipping to beat the band.

Back across the street, Willie leaned his bulk against the smokehouse door to keep the Germans in. But finally, they pushed their way out and peered into the night with chunks of wood raised up as clubs. They looked at Mari and then at Willie.

"Es ist ein kleines mädchen und ein grober ricker mann." It's a little girl and an oversized man. And they began to laugh.

Mari's stomach churned, and she looked desperately for some way to defend themselves.

Suddenly, neighbors appeared wielding brooms, rakes, bats, and even a hockey stick. When the dark-haired German brandished his club at Mari, Mama materialized, hefting a cast iron skillet. She attacked the German, jabbing him in the chest until he backed up and tripped over the smoldering wood pile.

When he fell, Willie charged. "He won't be going anywhere for a while," Willie said, sitting on the flailing German like a bull moose on a squirrel.

The other German looked stunned, and when Sgt. Pulver showed up with his partner, he simply raised his hands, ready for handcuffs.

It was quite a night, and everyone got up the next morning a little tired but satisfied.

Tuesday, Mama opened the newspaper.

Led by a spunky fifth grader who sounded the alarm, neighbors on Thirteenth Avenue captured the German prisoners who had eluded the police for the past several months. Willie Churlin of Churlin's Grocery was instrumental in detaining the most dangerous escapee, and the other prisoner simply gave up without a fight.

"It's really Moses who deserves the credit," Mari said of Miss Edith Fleming's cat. *"He and his sparring partner, Caruso, made such a loud fuss that our neighbors came over and surrounded the prisoners before they knew what was happening."*

The article went on, *Johnny and Peter Cmar are two of our brave fighting men, and Mari says she is proud to help her country in honor of her brothers and all the servicemen who are fighting overseas.*

The Accordion

Mari hated it. She didn't want it. She never, ever wanted it at all. But there was no arguing with Mama when Johnny brought home an accordion from Pinch-a-Penny Pawn. He had given it to brother Peter Jr. for a Christmas surprise before the war that year. Mari never supposed she would be the one who would end up surprised. Not only that Christmas, but all year long—one very long year.

Peter took up the instrument only once and squeezed out a note as long and sharp as a gas pain before he set it aside forever. "Never mind," Mama said, "Mari will play. It is just her size."

Mari looked at the thing, all pearly white with black bellows and twenty- four shiny white buttons, and asked why the family couldn't have a piano. She had been begging for that piano for over a year now.

"Costs too much money," Mama said and ended the argument right there. "In Europe, we call this a harmonium, my favorite instrument," she beamed.

But Mari wasn't buying that; she knew Mama's favorite instrument was really the mandolin or maybe even the balalaika. Mama could never let go of her old country ways.

Oh, she tried to be American. They all wanted to be "as American as apple pie!" So, Mama baked big apple pies and cut them into squares like brownies. She loved "Memrick" (Maverick) on TV and called Peter's friend Johnny Warieka "Walnuts," a name he carried until he died. But all along, Mari knew her family was different. They ate *rozki* instead of chocolate chip cookies and spoke only Lemko and Slavic at home. Their music was Tchaikovsky and Rimsky-Korsakov and Byzantine chant. Old-world saints in heavy frames peered at them from every room in the house. Mari was the only kid in her class who could recite the Cyrillic alphabet. In fact, Mari was cross-cultural before cross-culture was cool.

So, she learned to play the accordion. Not well. But she played.

Every Saturday afternoon, Mr. Evans, the egg man, would come to deliver fresh eggs from his farm a few miles from town. And every afternoon, even Saturdays, there she would be, practicing that accordion. One sunny fall day, Mari heard voices in the kitchen. Mama hurried into the front room, smiling, "Mr. Evans says you are playing so well, Mari, that he is inviting you to play at the Grange meeting next month. Farmers will come from all over the county for that meeting, and you will be the entertainment."

"I really don't think I can do that; I'm too scared to play in front of a group of strangers," Mari told her mother, stammering excuses and suddenly feeling a lump the size of a baseball in her throat.

"Well," said Mr. Evans, "Mari, you think on it. I'll come back next week. You could let me know then."

That week, Mama brought out her big guns. Mari's sisters said they could see she had real talent, and Mama thought she might put the blue dress she and Mari had seen in Goldblatt's window on Christmas layaway.

With all that pressure, Mari reluctantly agreed that she would play at the Grange. She felt her family's hopes lying heavily on her skinny, little shoulders.

When it was over, Mari would realize the performance had been a one-way ticket on the Titanic.

While she made really pretty music for a while, the last piece, some classical nightmare she had picked out to show off, seemed to come rolling faster and faster out of that accordion. Then her fingers parted company with her brain, and the music ended in a pitiful wheeze.

That night, Mari learned that farm people are very polite. Many came up to tell her what a fine girl she was and that her parents must be very proud of her. And they said it was "really spunky" for her to end the program with such a difficult piece of music. It was a fine effort, they said, and they could tell she would be a really fine accordion player one day.

Those nice farmers, God bless 'em, were wrong.

Wartime at the Steel Mill

The streetcar doors opened, and a load of men spilled out into the early morning darkness. Peter stepped down from the trolley and coughed as the icy air bit into the back of his throat. Turning up the collar of his sheepskin jacket, he moved with the others toward the steel mill entrance. Charley Gray fell in alongside him, and they walked at a brisk pace toward the hulking shadow of the plant. Charley was only twenty-two, but his bad leg made him 4-F. Despite this, he gimped along with surprising speed.

"Jesus, it's cold," Charley muttered and hunkered deeper into his jacket. Overhead, a single streetlight flickered, its feeble yellow light struggling against the darkness.

"It's a bitch, all right." Peter saw his breath coming in little puffs when he spoke. As they approached the bridge on their way to the gate, the incline grew steeper, and they could hear the river water lapping underneath. Bright lights along the bank showed inky water licking at the slabs of ice along the shoreline.

"I always feel like I'm crossing a moat, Pete."

"In the old days, that's what we called it, Charley. We called this river the moat. But back then, the river would have run right through the plant, so we moved it."

"The river? You moved the river?"

"We did. Before the plant was built, we moved this river a thousand feet south, diverted a two-mile stretch right here to where it is now."

"I heard the story but never knew if it was true. How? You use machines?" Charley's words were muffled because he was burrowed down in his coat.

"Nope. Horses. Horses pulling slip scoops. Long, hard days."

"How long did it take?"

"Two years. 'Course, we did it in warmer weather than this. In summer, we fought snakes, hornets, chiggers, and mosquitoes. God, it was hot. I wouldn't mind some of that heat right now," he said, sorry he hadn't taken the scarf Katya had tried to foist on him when he left the house.

"Look up ahead, Pete. Aren't there cops on the railroad bridge? Think there's a problem?"

"Just wartime security," Peter guessed. But there was no question the number of guards eyeing them from the railroad tracks had increased since yesterday.

"Something's up, Pete. Remember that fire in New York Harbor?"

"You mean when longshoremen were outfitting that big luxury ship for a troop transport and she caught fire and burned?"

"That one. FBI jumped on the case."

"That was New York, Charley."

"Yeah, but after that fire, we got new IDs with a picture, fingerprints, as well as height and weight. I tell you, something's up."

Maybe J. Edgar Hoover had issued some kind of alert. Plant security had been drilled into all of them since the war started. FBI warnings were posted throughout the plant. Bosses kept warning to be on the lookout for saboteurs. At first everyone was wary, but like everything else, after a while, all the warnings had become routine.

After the bridge, they headed into the tunnel beneath the railroad tracks. Peter pulled off one of his gloves and fumbled in his pocket for his badge. When they reached the gate, another cop was posted at the entrance. He kept blowing into his hands and stomping his feet to keep warm. Behind him, two National Guardsmen stood turtle-like, only their eyes visible above their coat collars. But those eyes kept traveling back and forth, scanning the line. When Peter stepped up to show his badge, he could feel the cold crawl past his wrist and into his sleeve. At the cop's curt nod, he moved inside, shoving the ID back into his pocket.

At the clock house, they fell into line all over again. Finally, they stepped inside, welcoming the short respite from the wind.

"Well, well. Lookee here, Pete! We got us a purty new poster tacked up on the wall."

Peter looked at a smiling young woman manning a drill press above the words, "We helped build our nation. We'll help them defend it."

"Humph! Never saw a woman who looks that good in my section," growled a big man up ahead, reaching out to punch the time clock.

"You get them to pay me a man's wages, and I'll buy a brand new outfit and curl my hair just for you," the solid forty-ish woman behind him cracked.

A couple of men snickered, but she ignored them and sashayed on ahead, ample hips straining her thick cloth coat with every step she took. She turned in at the far end of the building where a separate wash house had been jerry-rigged for the women now working at the plant. Before the war, females were very rarely seen on the factory floor, confined instead to the offices and, on occasion, to the lab. There had been no reason for them to shower after work. "Always wanted a look inside that other washhouse," the big man said mournfully. "But if they're all built like she is, I'll let it ride."

"You seen Gloria that works over in the Tin Mill?" Charley asked. "I got a buddy there says she's a real looker."

"If that's Lars Johnson's girl, I wouldn't mess with her," the big man offered. "Her father's first helper in the open hearth. Capice?"

"Well, a man can dream, can't he?"

The kid pushed open the door to the wash house, and Peter went over to one of the metal chains hanging from the ceiling and opened his padlock. The other men did likewise, each lowering his own metal basket.

"My buddy heard they got a couple of convicts working over at the main building," the big man said.

"The hell you say?" Peter pulled out his work clothes and laid them on the bench. He removed his coat and stuffed it into the basket. Stripping off his street clothes, he changed into work pants and a shirt before easing into his work jacket.

"That's what I heard. With all the draftees gone, they need more help."

"That why we need more security?"

"Nah. Those new guys are old, even older than you, Pete. One of them says he used to be a doctor."

"Sure. And I'm the queen of England," the big guy said.

Peter closed the lid on his basket, hoisting it back up to the ceiling. Charley waved and was gone, and Peter headed in the direction of the open hearth.

To warm up, he detoured past the soaking pits. Here, pig iron ingots rested in troughs of hot water on their way to other parts of the plant for processing. The place was a hell hole in summer, but Peter relished the heat on a morning like this.

Peter's job as a troubleshooter gave him a wider run of the mill than most. Through the years, he'd worked his way up from electrician to motor inspector. But it was his ear for languages that brought him to the bosses' attention in the first place. They found the friendly greenhorn a fluent interpreter for the Eastern Europeans who'd flocked to work in the plant. After a while, even old man Sturgill took notice and started calling him Jack-of- All-Trades, and, later, just Jack. Some of the old-timers still called him that.

During the First World War, the management had trucked in Mexicans to replace men who'd gone overseas. During Peter's old hell-raising days with Chick, he'd lived around Mexicans; they were his drinking buddies, and he'd picked up the lingo quickly. It came in handy when the doughboys left for the front. But when the war ended, they herded those same Mexicans into boxcars and warned they'd shoot them if they ever returned. So, the doughboys had their jobs back.

This war and this time around, Puerto Ricans were brought in as replacement workers. Mostly they had the shit jobs, and even though the dialect was different, Peter found he could translate just fine.

He could see the machine shop up ahead, and Gypsy, an apprentice, ground out his cigarette before he went back inside. Chico, one of the young Puerto Ricans, trotted up alongside Peter, and they hurried together to the shop.

Chico was his new helper, a transfer from the coke plant who barely spoke English. "Malo," he'd replied when Peter asked how it was over there. "Muy malo."

The coke plant was the dirtiest place in the mill. Peter had started there, himself. As a youngster, they'd put him to work shoveling the gray, pockmarked lumps of coke in the yard. After one shift, he'd told the boss he'd had enough. He would do anything else, shovel anywhere in the mill, but he'd take his pink slip rather than go back to the coke plant. By some miracle, they'd moved him the next day.

Inside the machine shop, the boss was waiting for him. "Number two crane. It's down again, Pete."

Peter wouldn't have minded a cup of hot coffee; he eyed the pot on the burner but knew it would have to wait. "That's the second time this week."

"Yeah. And the foreman is cussin' like a sailor. He wants you. Pronto."

Peter motioned to Chico and then went to unlock his toolbox, removing a flashlight, continuity tester, and a few other tools. He tucked them into his toolbelt, and both of them threaded their way through the scrapyard to the far side of the furnace.

In the yard, they could see Harold, who'd climbed down from his steam shovel, jawing away at the new helper, Vinnie, who was jawing right back. The war had meant some shifting around the yard, and Harold and Vinnie had been thrown together, but they'd rubbed each other the wrong way from the start. Peter heard the word "arbitrator" and hurried away. Any arbitrator assigned to those two would have his work cut out for him.

Peter had his own work to do, and he was tired. He'd been fighting a cold all week, and there had been a rash of problems lately. But anyone who worked around men and machines could tell you that, eventually, one or the other was bound to break down.

Wartime made everything worse. Foremen, pushing hard, bore down on men tired from putting in so many extra hours. The machines ran twenty-four hours a day, seven days a week.

Sometimes the men got careless. It was the monotony. And sometimes a lazy night crew would purposely throw a little sand in a machine to stop it so the guys could get some quiet sleep.

The machines all needed regular maintenance. Every once in a while, somebody tried a shortcut, but it didn't work. You needed to stay with the routine. The machines rarely gave out, all things considered, but last week had been one for the books. Peter coughed and reached into his pocket for a handkerchief. He blew his nose and hurried to where the overhead crane was down. The trolley house was empty.

"How lovely you could make it, Jack." Stan, the foreman, sneered down from the gantry, the big structure that supported the crane. He was agitated, to say the least. "Last shift was playin' around up there for a long time. See what you can do, will you?"

Before going up, Peter checked the switch to see that the power was off. A small metal sign, "Maintenance. Do Not Activate Without Authorization," hung on a nail beside the box, but Peter fished out his own padlock and inserted it into the metal ring as insurance. Back in the old days, only a foreman could immobilize the switch, but one day, a new repairman hit a live cable, and they all watched his blackened body fall in a heap at their feet.

As Peter climbed the ladder, a cold, gray light was threading its way across the sky. The wind wasn't strong, but it stung his face as he climbed. He made his way toward the crane that had been loading scrap into the charging cars— railroad cars that carried scrap to the main floor to charge the furnaces. He felt chilled. In times past, a shot of whiskey would have warmed him, and his belly felt the familiar twinge. It had been two years since he'd touched a drop, but it didn't matter. He still craved it on occasion. He pushed the urge aside but knew it would be back again. "What's the problem, Peewee?"

Peewee Hardaway took off his glove and reached into his pocket for a handkerchief. He honked into it and looked at Peter with reddened eyes. "We got power up to this point,

Pete, but from here, I don't know where she shorted out. The rest is up to you."

"Where's the operator?"

"In the can. I said it was okay since we was shut down, anyway."

Peter retrieved his flashlight and moved to the narrow platform encircling the machine. "We had trouble here last week, Peewee. I made a splice a little farther down, but it could have shorted out again."

He was working his way along the cable when the operator came back up. He was surprised to see the woman from the clock house.

"Name's Astrid," she said and swung easily into the trolley house. "Let me know when you want me to rev her up."

"Trouble's not where I thought," Peter said. "We have to keep working our way around."

With Chico holding the light, they inched their way around the machine, but it took a while before they finally managed to locate the break.

"That ought to do it," Peter said, straightening up and working one knee to get the kink out of the joint.

"I'll go down and give you some juice, Astrid, then we'll see if she's running okay."

They climbed back down, and Peter went to remove the padlock. Flipping the switch, he looked up. Slowly, the machine began to lumber toward the pile of scrap. Lowering the big magnet at the end of the cable, it attached the load, swung it over, and dumped it all into the railroad car.

Astrid leaned out of the trolley house and snapped off a salute. Peter thought he could make out a smile. He tipped his cap as the machine reached into the pile for another bite.

Back in the shop, he took some time to warm up and then took a burned-out motor down from the shelf. Gypsy bent over for a look, puffing on his Lucky Strike. Chico had gone to the can. "How was it?" Gypsy asked.

"He did fine."

"I seen a woman in the trolley house. And to top it off, now we got us a Spic helper. Ain't no place for a Spic. Why ain't he on a shovel?"

"Because it's wartime, Gypsy. That's why."

"I don't like working with Spics."

"Well, maybe he doesn't like Gypsies, either," Peter grunted, referring to the dark good looks that had earned Gypsy his nickname. "Chico learns quick. He does fine."

"Well, I don't like it."

Peter straightened up and tried to work the crick out of his back. Gypsy was testier than usual lately. He must be having trouble with his woman again. Peter knew he missed his euchre. Before the war, they might wait an hour, sometimes three, before being called out on a job. And, if there were no small motors to repair and no urgent maintenance, Gypsy was always looking for a game of euchre.

Everything was different now, and Gypsy wasn't a happy man. "Rumor has it the mill is running short of coal. You heard anything, Pete?"

"Just what I read in the newspaper." They had all been following the wildcat strikes in the coal fields. John L. Lewis, the bushy-browed president of the CIO (Congress of Industrial Organizations), kept threatening a general strike if his miners couldn't get a decent wage.

"Those poor bastards are always on the hind end of everything. Explosions, lousy pay. I wouldn't work in those filthy holes for nothing."

True. The mill might be dirty and noisy, and it could be dangerous as well, but it was above ground. Peter had a lot of sympathy for the miners. They all did. However, coal strikes threatened war production, and the troops needed steel to end the war. And Peter wanted his two sons back home again.

"We got us a problem over by the open hearth," Gypsy said.

Peter took the work order and gathered up his tools; soon, they were on their way again. They were busy all day long. Only the noon whistle reminded him it was dinnertime. Chico ran back to the shop for their lunch buckets, and they ate on the job.

166

Ten hours later, Peter stepped out of the wash house and back into the darkness. He made his way toward the streetcar line and climbed aboard, grateful for the empty seat. A hot shower had removed most of the grime and some of the stiffness, but the long day had left him weary. He could hear his stomach growl. Katya would be waiting to heat up his supper when he got home, but he knew he'd be too tired to eat much.

"Go to work in the dark. Come home in the dark. How long since you seen the sun, Pete?" Astrid had wedged herself into the seat next to him. "But I'm not complaining. I tried for a long time to get a job at the mill."

Peter grunted and made a point of looking out the window. He wouldn't mind some peace and quiet.

"The mill's the only place a woman can make some real money. Not what a man makes, but still good money."

They were nearing downtown, and patches of snow here and there were the only relief among the varied grays of the darkened buildings.

"And I needed the work, see? Chalk it all up to my dear, departed husband."

"When did he die?"

"Oh, he didn't die. He just departed. Took off five years ago, and I haven't seen him since." She barked out a laugh and slapped him on the knee. "Gotcha good that time, didn't I?" And when he didn't answer, asked, "You married, Pete?"

"'Fraid so."

"I could tell."

He was getting uncomfortable from the way she was looking at him. She had the same look old man Churlin did when he was eyeing a prime beef carcass in his cooler.

"I like running a crane, too. Been around machines all my life. I was raised on a farm."

In the window reflection, Peter could see Astrid's head scarf had fallen down around her shoulders. She didn't bother to pull it up but patted the braids that wound around her head in a crown.

"My family didn't start out as farmers. When Grandad came over from Sweden, work was scarce. He got a job packing dynamite into shell casings at the explosives factory over in the sand dunes."

"That plant where the blast blew a hole in the door of a grade school a mile away?"

"That's the one. One day, Grandad saw this man next to him lift some dynamite from a pallet. The powder exploded and killed him on the spot. Grandad was spared, but he was deaf as a stone from then on. He walked out of that factory and never looked back. That's when he turned to farming."

"Halfway point. Madison Street," the conductor called.

A couple of men got off. In his drinking days, Peter would get off here. Halfway Point was halfway to the end of the line. That meant you paid only half fare and had a nickel left over for a glass of beer. That's how Peter had justified stopping off at Whitey's for all those years. He wouldn't mind getting off even now to warm the empty spot in his belly.

"I heard you were Catholic."

There she was, eyeing him again. Where had she been getting all this information?

"I should have married a Catholic. They don't believe in divorce, do they? If my man had been Catholic, he might have stayed around longer."

"My stop," he said, relieved when they'd made it to Grant Street. When he reached up to pull the cord, Astrid moved into the aisle to let him pass. He stepped outside into the frigid air and walked the two blocks home.

Miss Gary War Bonds

Helen hurried toward the streetcar line. Catching her slender, leggy image in Woolworth's window, she pulled her shoulders back and lifted her head higher. "Miss Gary War Bonds," she breathed, her long auburn hair swaying with each high-heeled stride. She could feel the butterflies skittering in her stomach. Barely an hour earlier, Mr. Bear had called her into his office to tell her that Bear Brand Hosiery had selected her, line-seamstress and parachute finisher Helen Cmar, as its official entry in the Miss Gary War Bonds Pageant.

"This contest will generate donations for the war effort, Miss Cmar," Mr. Bear intoned from behind his massive desk. "Our troops need weapons, clothing, supplies. Oh, we can have our scrap drives," he said, waving a dismissive hand, "and donate our old tires and cooking grease, but war bonds raise cash, and cash is king! Other cities have had great success with similar efforts. I'm sure you will do us proud."

With the barest sniff, old Miss Pocock, his longtime executive secretary, gave Helen the entry form to fill out and bring back tomorrow.

On the ride home, she couldn't resist jiggling her knees up and down, anticipating Mama's surprise when she heard what had happened. And she couldn't wait to see the envy in MaryAnn's eyes. She pulled the cord to stop the car and fairly flew the two blocks to the house. In the kitchen, Mama and MaryAnn sat with their heads together in earnest conversation.

"Oh, Helen, we've been waiting for you!"

"I know I'm late, but Mr. Bear called me into his office after work."

"Sit down. MaryAnn has big news."

"Not really, not that big," MaryAnn said modestly. But her eyes sparked a different story.

"Of course it is. Tell your sister."

"Well, you're looking at Sears' entry in, well, I guess a beauty contest."

"We could be looking at Miss Gary War Bonds," Mama beamed.

Helen looked at her sister, who was all but purring. "You?"

"Yes. Can you believe it?"

"Well, I mean, you might be considered pretty and all, but I never pictured you in a beauty contest."

"I never did, either," MaryAnn said, lowering her eyes.

Suddenly, it irritated Helen to no end when MaryAnn gave her that dopey, "aren't we humble" look.

"They called me into the executive offices right after lunch, Helen. The department heads were all there. I thought I'd done something wrong," she giggled. "But the big boss asked if I would like to be Miss Sears War Bonds and compete for the city title."

"And she told them yes!" Mama said.

"Well, not at first, I didn't. I was so surprised. In my own mind, I've never been the beauty contest sort."

"But you're married!" Helen felt betrayed. Here was MaryAnn's husband fighting overseas, and what did his bride do? She agreed to start running around, enjoying herself in some contest.

"They know I'm married. They said it didn't matter."

"So, you just up and agreed!" Helen huffed.

"Well, no. Not at first. But Mr. Carlin said the executives all voted for me. He said I was their unanimous choice. I didn't want to seem ungrateful."

Helen wondered if she had been the unanimous choice at Bear Brand Hosiery or simply Mr. Bear's choice because it was his company. She saw him watching her sometimes as she moved through the factory, and he'd even put his hand on her arm, pretending to show her how to adjust her machine.

"What about you, Helen? Any news? You looked happy when you came in. Did the new guy at the plant talk to you today?"

"No, he didn't talk to me. And yes, I have news."

"Tell us." Mama rose to turn down the flame under the vegetable soup on the stove.

"It's nothing." Helen slumped, arms crossed, into her chair.

170

"Come on. We're listening."

"You're just looking at the Bear Brand Hosiery contestant for Miss Gary War Bonds. That's all."

"You're kidding!" MaryAnn squealed and rushed over to her. She grabbed both her hands and tried to pull her up. Helen didn't budge. "That's wonderful, Sis! And you'll probably win too, as pretty as you are."

Helen looked at MaryAnn and then at Mama and tried to smile. She really did. But the joy had faded. *Not fair,* she thought. *My one big chance, and I have to pretend to be glad my sister's in the same pageant.*

Mama hugged her and said she was proud, but Helen felt like a deflated balloon. Feigning a headache, she clomped upstairs to her small attic bedroom.

The dressing table skirt was bunched to one side, so she straightened it, and then, peering into the mirror, she fluffed the cluster of Betty Grable curls on her forehead. She pulled a record out of its paper jacket and placed it on the turntable. Cranking the handle, she laid the needle down, and a silky male voice began to croon, "Marie Elena, you're the answer to my prayer."

The portable phonograph had been her splurge, but it was worth it. She rubbed a hand over the genuine imitation leather case, a bargain even though it had cost half of her week's salary. Twelve-fifty well spent.

Kicking aside the movie magazines scattered on the floor, she went over and opened the window under the eaves, watching her filmy curtains take flight in the autumn breeze. Stripping down to panties and brassiere, she slipped her falsies out of each bra cup and laid them on the dressing table.

Victor Mature smiled up at her from the cover of *Silver Screen Magazine.* She picked it up and gazed at the movie star, at his thick, wavy hair, dark eyes, and full, sensuous mouth smiling a come-hither smile.

"Victor, you can put your shoes under my bed anytime," she murmured dreamily. MaryAnn scolded her when she said things like that, so she smiled and said it again.

171

Idly flipping magazine pages, she read about the stars who attended a glamorous cocktail party. On the opposite page, a young starlet leaned provocatively into the camera. The Movie Magic pageant winner told how her contest had raised a record amount of money for war bonds. Helen pored over the details of the contest, turning back to read the article one more time before she closed her eyes and drifted off.

"To share this love is really all I ask of you ..." she didn't hear the final words of the song or the rhythmic scratching of the needle as the machine ground slowly to a halt.

A few days later, she went into the kitchen after work to see MaryAnn at the table, one leg thrust high in the air.

"This, Mama, is the perfect leg. When the man from the contest took my measurements at work today, he said my leg is the perfect size."

"Well, la-di-dah!" Helen said, mincing into the kitchen.

"Oh, hi, Sis." Blushing, MaryAnn dropped her leg and adjusted her skirt. "Well, I guess I *am* bragging, but everyone here always says I'm too skinny, so it was nice to hear someone say I'm perfectly proportioned. Did they take your measurements yet?"

"Yes," Helen mumbled and flounced out of the room. Early yesterday morning, a man armed with a tape measure was waiting with Miss Pocock inside her office. Under the secretary's watchful eye, he took Helen's measurements, made a quick record, and remembered to tip his hat before he left.

In her room, she plopped on her bed with a sigh. Here she was, twenty-seven years old, her life on hold until the right man came along. But all the good ones were off fighting the war, and no one could tell how long the war would last.

The next week, all the girls had their pictures taken. Helen's night was Thursday. The winner's photo would be mailed to the Gary boys overseas to remind them what they were fighting for. Well, she'd show them, all right. She posed in a leopard-print bathing suit and high heels. Hands on her hips, she stood with her back to the camera. Then, a la Betty Grable, she peeked back over her shoulder at the photographer. When he told her she looked just like the movie star, she whispered, "Eat dirt, Miss Perfect Measurements."

How could she know the newspaper would run that picture one week later? She heard Mama's gasp when she opened the paper and watched her trying to hide the section before Papa came to breakfast. What kind of daughter, Mama demanded, would take a picture barely dressed like that? They could never hold their heads high in Churlin's Grocery ever again!

Papa weighed in later, saying didn't she know exposing her limbs like that would make men think she was "loose"?

Still, it wasn't a bad article, she thought. It made much of the fact that two sisters were competing in the same pageant. It showed MaryAnn in a black strapless evening gown, a gardenia in her long dark hair. "Though this contestant is married," the article explained, "contest rules do not specify marital status."

"Her sister," according to the entry form, "enjoys the single life and lists her age as twenty-two."

Helen was glad to escape the house and her parents' tirade that morning. Slipping into her chair at the factory, she adjusted her machine, ready to help turn the new reams of silk into chutes for men at the front. Though it was still called Bear Brand Hosiery, the plant had switched from silk stockings to making parachutes. Silk, a precious commodity, wouldn't be available to civilians until after the war.

Fat Harry, the foreman at work, came up and rattled the morning paper in her ear. "'The purpose of this competition,'" he read, "'is to generate interest in buying war bonds.' It generates interest, all right," he leered, glancing at the photo and then at her, "but it sure ain't in no war bonds." He clamped his cigar between his teeth and waddled off, chuckling.

"Papa was right," she sighed. She vowed to concentrate solely on the day's parachute quota.

None of the girls at the plant said much to her all that week, but she could see them casting sidelong glances in her direction and talking among themselves. Then one day, Sophie, the inspector down the line, complained loudly that someone's work was growing slipshod. She had to turn some pieces over to the reject pile. And she could guess whose work it was. "But I know it won't do to complain," she added, "since I'm just one of the girls. Not Mr. Bear's pick for Miss Gary War Bonds."

The new finisher also started making insinuating remarks, but when she tried to tell Harry, he just laughed it off. The girls she usually ate lunch with drifted off by themselves and the new man she had hoped would notice her had been fired.

Later, during the ten-minute morning break, she dashed to the front office and tried to talk to Miss Pocock about what to do. But she was no help at all, sitting with her lips pressed together while Helen laid out her story.

"So, you have reaped the whirlwind, have you?"

"Whirlwind? No, there's no whirlwind. I just don't know what to do."

"Short of dropping out, you mean?"

"Of the contest?" Helen was horrified. "Oh, I couldn't do that!"

Then Miss Pocock adjusted the cameo at her throat and murmured something about Shakespeare and those who have greatness thrust upon them.

"Miss Pocock ....,"

But Miss Pocock had risen from the desk. The interview was over.

MaryAnn wasn't saying much to her these days, and Mama was unusually quiet, as well. *I'll be glad when this damn contest is over,* she thought, longing for the easy camaraderie they had always enjoyed. The days were getting shorter, too, and the long, dark nights only matched her mood.

The night of the contest finally arrived. There was a nip in the air as MaryAnn drove them both in Rick's old Ford coupe to the high school. It felt odd to be driving because gas rationing meant the car could be used only sparingly. A makeup case lay between them on the seat, and Helen held both MaryAnn's formal and her own bathing suit on her lap.

"Are you nervous?" MaryAnn asked.

"No," she lied.

"I am," MaryAnn said, rounding the corner. "I'm nervous as a cat. I don't actually like doing this, but the people at work have been so kind, I couldn't think of backing out."

"Must be great having nice people at work."

Neither said anything more then, and they drove along in silence for a while.

"I hope you win, Helen. I know you want to."

"I hope I win, too. It will help me get what I want."

They pulled into the high school parking lot and carried their clothes inside. Other contestants were already crowded into the bathroom.

"Don't you think a lot of these girls are really pretty?" Helen whispered, looking around anxiously. She slipped into one of the stalls and changed into her bathing suit. After helping each other with hair and makeup, they were herded into another room where a toothy woman gave instructions. Most girls wore bathing suits; only MaryAnn and one other girl had opted for formals.

They drew the order of appearance from numbered papers in a jar. MaryAnn drew number four. "Good. I'll get it over with," she breathed. Helen squeezed her hand in reassurance before reaching in to pull out her own number: eighteen, second to last. They marched in their order to the gymnasium door.

A makeshift stage had been set up at one end of the floor. Four judges sat at a table facing that stage, their backs to the audience. The contestants were to slowly parade in front of the table, leaving time for each judge to mark their ballot and for the audience to get a good look at each girl as she crossed.

Behind the judges, the first two rows of audience chairs were ribboned off and empty. A man from the radio station was busy setting up his equipment. Another man with a fedora tilted back on his head, slouched in his seat, writing in a notepad. He had to be from the newspaper—maybe the same one who had written the article about them. The toothy woman at the door pointed out prominent citizens as people filtered into the gym.

175

A man went to the microphone and raised a hand to signal it was time to start. "Good evening, ladies and gentlemen."

"Miss Toothy" hurried her final instructions in a low voice. "Girls, there will be two rounds. In the first round, you parade slowly past the judges, walk to the other side of the stage area, turn, and walk back again. Remember, you must walk slowly. Then the judges will confer among themselves and pick five finalists. Now, off you go! And remember: smile big, and don't let the photographer's flashbulbs distract you."

Then they were off and running. "Contestant Number One. Number Two. Three. Number Four." Then there was a pause and a flurry of confusion. "Attention, young ladies! We call again for Contestant Number Four." MaryAnn stood frozen, so Helen gave her a quick hug and then pushed her onto the stage.

"So petite," someone whispered. "I wonder what size she wears."

"Looks like the movie version of the girl next door."

And so it went.

"Contestant Number Eighteen."

Helen swept into the room and was surprised to hear a sprinkling of applause. "Atta girl, Betty Grable!" someone yelled from the back. The audience rippled with laughter, and she turned a bright smile to the crowd. *I could get used to this,* she thought. A couple of wolf whistles emboldened her along the way, and she kicked up a heel before sashaying offstage.

Round One was over in a heartbeat, but the judges' decision seemed to stretch into an eternity. She held her breath as they finally announced the names. "Delinsky, O'Brien, Vovich, Demarko, and Number Five, Helen Cmar.

All but the five finalists were ushered back into the gym to fill the empty chairs in front. MaryAnn managed a thumbs up to Helen before she went to sit behind the judges.

"Finalist number Five."

Walking out to even more applause, Helen took her time, sauntered to the far end of the stage, turned, and walked back to the judges' table. She offered a languid smile, placed both palms on the surface, and leaned very slowly and sensuously toward the men.

"Woah, Nellie!" the oldest judge exclaimed, obviously perplexed. The judge next to him gawked and turned away. MaryAnn, in the first row, was making frantic gestures.

Confused, Helen stood up quicker than she intended. *What is she doing?* Helen thought angrily. Then she heard the young judge snicker. What could be wrong? Bewildered, Helen bolted from the stage.

The other finalists were clustered together in the doorway, and she saw Miss Toothy making a beeline in her direction. But as Miss Toothy was about to tell Helen what had happened, the winner was announced.

"And the winner is ... Miss Cookie Delinsky!"

Helen stood blinking back tears when MaryAnn hurried up behind her. "It's your falsies, Helen. They've worked their way up out of your bathing suit!"

Helen looked down. Horrified, she pushed each of the culprits back down into her swimsuit. "I've never been so humiliated," she said later when they climbed into the car.

"It was just an accident," MaryAnn consoled. "And not many people could see."

"Really?"

"Yes. I just happened to be in the front row. Still, I think it's a shame. Otherwise, you would have won."

"You think so," Helen sniffed. "I don't just *think* so. I *know.*"

The next morning, the paper listed Helen Cmar, Miss Bear Brand War Bonds, as one of the finalists. In the front office, Mr. Bear, with Miss Pocock at his side, called her in to offer his congratulations. While he and Mrs. Bear did not attend the program, he said, "Mrs. Bear not holding truck with beauty contests," he was nonetheless pleased with the way Helen had represented the company. Being one of the five finalists, he said, was a feather in all their caps. He was pleased to offer her a twenty-five-dollar war bond for her efforts.

Life went back to normal after that—as normal as life could be during wartime. Helen was no closer to finding the right man. She'd just have to wait until the war was over. "But by then, I'll be ancient," she groaned. Back at work, she was one of the girls again, and Mama said it was something to be a finalist, wasn't it?

A month later, there was a letter from Johnny with heavily censored news from overseas. But then he went on and on about the newspaper picture MaryAnn had sent. He showed the picture to the guys, and they all wanted a date with Helen. Several even asked if they could write to her. And one, a Texan, vowed to look her up as soon as he got back to the States.

In that sense, the contest was a success. But as she told MaryAnn later, when it came to Miss Pocock and Shakespeare and that nonsense about greatness thrust upon you … well, as far as she was concerned, it wasn't worth a thimbleful of spit.

Helen and Willie at the Starlight Terrace

Yawning, Helen raised her arms above her head, arched her back, and stretched catlike on her bed. When the movie magazine she was holding hit the bedpost and slithered to the floor, she didn't bother to retrieve it. "Who cares about starlets surrounded by adoring servicemen, anyway?"

Helen was more than usually depressed this Saturday morning. Thrusting her lower lip into a pout, she contemplated her life. There was her boring job with all those other women at Bear Brand Hosiery. There was night after lonely night with no telephone calls. Why, lately, she'd even found herself jealous of MaryAnn, who was always mooning over how much she missed Rick. At least MaryAnn had someone. But she, Helen, was manless, adrift like a ship without a rudder on the barren seas of the home front.

For reassurance, she reached for her mirror and peered into it for a while, fluffing up the bird's nest of curls on her forehead. Finally, she put the mirror down again and sighed. "What's the good of being good-looking when there's a war on." Turning her face to the wall, she mourned the monotony of her life.

The excitement of the Miss Gary War Bonds contest was long past, and the only one who ever mentioned it these days was Fat Harry, the foreman. Once in a while, he still called her "the beauty queen" or brought up the time she'd won "that glamour whatsis." While the references did build up her ego, Helen couldn't help but cringe at the way Harry leered at her when he said it.

Later that night, Helen decided to cast aside her melancholia to give her love life one last chance. She went with her friend Tillie to Danceland.

"Have you ever seen so many uniforms?" Tillie breathed, trying to shove a brassiere strap back under her dress. "What kind do you like best?"

"The navy uniform is my favorite," Helen smiled, batting her eyes at a passing sailor. He took the bait and swept her into his arms and onto the floor. But when he clutched her to him in a kind of death grip and kept panting into her ear, Helen realized she'd made a mistake. As soon as the song was over, she murmured some excuse and got away. Three other servicemen came up to her, one after another. The first was awkward, the second boring, and the third somehow managed to be both.

She made her way back to Tillie and pulled her into a corner. "How are we supposed to make conversation with guys we've never seen before?"

"Helen, you've done it plenty of times."

"This is different. I've always known at least a few people here."

"There's a war on, remember? The guys we know have already shipped out."

"That's just it. All our friends are gone. We won't see the guys here tonight until God knows when. Maybe never. I keep wondering if whichever guy I'm dancing with is dancing his last tango." She could tell from the look on Tillie's face that the disturbing notion wasn't hers alone. "Well, it's true, isn't it?"

"Helen, we've come here to show our boys a good time before they go off to war. It's our patriotic duty."

"Well, I don't want to waste my time wondering if everyone I'm dancing with is dancing his final waltz. This war business has certainly ruined Danceland, if you ask me."

"Oh, come on. I've never seen you so down. Snap out of it. Why, this could be your night, the night you find your one true love."

"Hey, Gorgeous. Remember me?"

Helen's breath caught in her throat at the sound of that voice. She turned around to look into the flashing brown eyes of Joey Dressel.

"It's me, Babe. Just got out of Basic. How do you like the new threads?" He spun around.

Helen felt faint. The acknowledged leader of the Danceland regulars was right there in front of her, all spit and polish in his uniform. She took in the confident thrust of his chin and the shining black hair slicked straight back from his forehead. "Joey, you look snappy!"

He shrugged and held out a hand. "Dance?"

Heads turned as they hit their stride in the jitterbug. Though they'd danced together before, Helen being one of the few who could keep up with him, Joey had never asked her out on a date. For a long time that was fine with her. What with Papa drinking, she didn't want anyone at the house, anyway. But now she could kick herself. She could have arranged to meet him somewhere.

"I'd almost forgotten what a great little dancer you are."

Oh, why hadn't she made a play for him before? Well, because there'd always been so many other guys around her. And Joey didn't dog her every step the way the rest of them did. But now she felt acute remorse. The next dance was slow, and he held her close. He laid his cheek against hers. They danced all the rest of the dances together.

"Be back in a flash," Joey told her at intermission. When he returned, he was holding a hand behind his back. "Three guesses … and the first two don't count."

"I couldn't imagine," Helen breathed, certain he'd bought her a corsage from the counter up at the front.

He held out a set of car keys. "My buddy's car's in the lot. He's got a bottle of hooch tucked into the upholstery in the back seat. Whattya say?"

"What are you talking about?"

"Look, Helen, it's my last night. I thought you and I could go outside. I watched you dancing with all those other guys. I could hardly stand it." Joey had come up close, hooked his finger into her neckline, and was peering down her dress. She jerked away.

"The back seat's big, Helen. Really comfortable." His gaze was earnest.

"Joey, what's gotten into you?"

"Aw, come on. It's my last night. I'm going overseas to do my patriotic duty. At a time like this, you should consider your duty, too."

When Joey laid his hand on her breast, Helen smacked it away and told him then and there what he could do with his hootch and his big back seat. She turned on her heel and stomped out of the hall. "Teach him to think I'm a one-night stand!"

She was so mad that she pushed the outside door hard enough to smack into the figure on the other side.

"Helen?"

There was Willie Churlin, his florid face breaking into a foolish grin. "Helen, I can't believe my luck in running into you like this."

Seeing the red welt that was beginning to puff up over Willie's eye, Helen wondered at his choice of words. "Willie, what are you doing here? I've never seen you at Danceland before."

"Well, I guess because this is my first time."

"I never realized someone like you could … I mean that you … cared to dance."

"Well, I guess there's a first time for everything." He grinned sheepishly.

"Willie, I'm sorry. I didn't mean it to come out like that."

"I know, Helen. It's okay."

She rubbed her hands over her arms.

"It's chilly out here, Helen. You should go back inside."

"I wouldn't go back in there for all the tea in China!"

Through the glass doors, they could see couples clinging together, swaying to the music.

"Then could I take you home?"

She almost laughed. Helen wondered what MaryAnn or her friends at work would think if they knew she had gone home from Danceland with the fat man from the grocery store. She shifted slightly. Her feet were aching in high heels.

"My car's over there." He indicated a big Buick. The car looked sleek and comfortable. Helen didn't relish the long, chilly walk to the streetcar line. Her evening had been ruined, anyway. But going home with Willie Churlin? It was out of the question.

"If you're leaving alone, why don't I give you a ride?"

Tillie! In a rush of gratitude, Helen remembered her friend. The two of them could ride home with Willie, and everything would be fine. That way, the ride was simply a lift, a convenience. Nothing more. Even MaryAnn couldn't make anything of that.

"I came with a friend. I'll go back and get her." Willie's face fell, but he managed a smile. "Sure. Swell. I'll wait right here for you."

Helen went back inside and found Tillie, who'd decided to go home with some boy in a Coast Guard uniform. Try as she might, she couldn't persuade her to change her mind. She could see Joey dancing slowly with a blonde in a tight dress. He looked over at her and then pulled the blonde even closer. That did it. What nerve! *Good riddance,* she sniffed and grabbed her wrap before running back outside.

The Buick was parked at the front curb, and Willie heaved himself out of his seat and went around to open the door.

"Nice car," Helen said, running her hand over the fine leather seat. Funny, she'd never noticed that Willie had such a fancy car. But then, she'd barely noticed him at all. "How can you drive this, what with the rationing and all?"

"Essential business use," he told her, spinning the radio dial.

Helen leaned back into the thick seat and was soon tapping her toes to Woody Herman's big band doing "String of Pearls." She had to admit this was cushier than running for the streetcar.

"Would you care to stop for something? It's late. I thought you might need a bite to eat."

She nearly panicked. Out on a date with Willie Churlin? "No! I couldn't eat a thing. Really."

"The Starlight Terrace serves a wonderful late supper. It's on our way. Well, not too far out of our way." He laughed at his own joke.

"Starlight Terrace?" She'd heard of it, of course. "I heard Frank Sinatra had dinner there once."

"He did. They have his photograph on the wall. Signed and everything."

"Really?"

"There are other movie stars, too. It's a well-known place."

"Do they have Gregory Peck?"

"Gregory Peck? I'm not sure about him."

"Gregory Peck enlisted, you know. He didn't have to, being a movie star and all. He could have stayed out, been safe, and made movies, but he enlisted. He's a captain in Special Forces."

"I'm not sure they have Gregory Peck."

Helen's thoughts were racing. What if somebody saw her out with Willie? What would that do to her reputation? But she'd heard so much about the Starlight Terrace. None of her boyfriends ever took her there since they couldn't afford it. To go to the same place where movie stars actually ate ....

"I think there's a wall in back I haven't seen," Willie added hopefully. "They could have Gregory Peck."

Oh, what was she worried about? Nobody Helen knew ever went to the Starlight Terrace.

"I think I *am* a little hungry, after all."

Willie turned the car in the opposite direction, and they drove to the supper club. He pulled up under the canopy at the front, where a uniformed doorman was waiting to help Helen from the car.

"Evening, George."

"Evening, Sir. I'll take good care of her." The doorman all but caressed the Buick's shiny black fender as Willie handed him the keys.

Inside, Willie indicated a luxuriously papered hallway. "The powder room is that way if you'd care to freshen up first."

Locating a door that said Les Mademoiselles, Helen found herself in the fanciest bathroom she'd ever seen. She chose one of the stalls and then went out to gaze at the crystal perfume bottles gleaming on the marble counter. She chose the biggest, fanciest bottle and sprayed a healthy dose behind each ear. After rinsing her hands, she stood looking around for the towel dispenser.

"Put some water behind your ears."

Helen jumped. "Oh, my goodness! You startled me."

"Rinse behind your ears," the thick black woman in front of her repeated. "You loaded on too much perfume, Honey. If you don't wash some of it off, you're gonna smell like a regular floozie."

Helen took in the motherly figure in the maid's uniform. She hesitated but then did as she was told. She took the soft little towel that was pressed into her hand.

"Where did you come from? I didn't know anyone else was in here?"

"Over there." The woman indicated an ornate gold chair in the corner.

"Well ... thanks."

The woman nodded toward a glass dish on the counter. It held three dollar bills and a few coins.

Helen paused and then fished around in her purse for her streetcar fare. "It's all I've got," she said and fled back to the dining room.

A tall man in a tuxedo stepped forward. "Right this way. Mr. Churlin is waiting at his usual table."

"He called you Mr. Churlin, Willie," Helen whispered, clearly impressed, as she slid into the opposite side of the booth. "Do you come here a lot?"

"Not a lot," he shrugged. "Would you like something to drink?"

"Cherry Coke, please," she told the waiter who had come up beside them. She looked around at the people, noticing how elegantly the women were dressed. The two at the next table were wearing long gowns.

Willie ordered a lobster salad with toast points for both of them.

"That's a nice perfume you're wearing, Helen. I hadn't noticed it before. It's subtle."

"Thank you. I've always said that too much perfume makes a girl smell cheap."

She couldn't get over the enormous black ceiling sprinkled with hundreds of lights that twinkled like stars above them.

And the velour upholstery was so thick it was almost like sitting on a cloud.

"I didn't know they had all-girl bands, Willie."

"They do now. Too many guys going off to fight."

She wanted to ask why he wasn't going but decided it wouldn't be polite to ask. She looked at Willie. Sitting down like this, with the table hiding his bulk, she saw his face was big, but his skin was smooth and his hair a rather nice shade of blonde. They had baked Alaska for dessert.

"I've never had baked Alaska before," she confessed. "I never even knew what it was."

She noticed that two young officers seated with posh women at the next table kept looking at them. Why were they scowling? Helen couldn't be sure but thought she heard the words "draft dodger."

Willie motioned to the waiter. When he came over, Willie pulled something out of his wallet and handed it to him, nodding at the two couples.

"Right away, Mr. Churlin." The waiter hurried away.

Not long afterward, Helen saw the waiter approach the next table and ceremoniously set a napkin before each of the men. Then he placed what looked like a glass of water beside it. Finally, he laid something small beside each glass and nodded over at Willie. There was a loud guffaw.

"Rap-a-Jap cocktails!" they bawled and, laughing, turned to raise their glasses to Willie.

Willie hoisted his in return. "My compliments to our fighting men."

Soon, the waiter was back with a bona fide cocktail for everyone at the table, and he indicated Willie again.

Clearly impressed, the men raised their glasses. "Damned nice of you, fella."

"Just because they kept me out of the service doesn't mean I don't back our fighting men one hundred percent."

"You Four-F?"

"Yep. Bad Ticker."

"Tough luck."

"You'll never know how tough," Willie replied sadly.

Helen leaned over and whispered. "What's a Rap-a-Jap cocktail, Willie?"

"It's a napkin, a glass of water, and a twenty-five-cent savings stamp."

Helen never knew Willie could manage things so well. "Is it true, Willie? That you tried to get in, I mean?" Helen was really interested now.

"You'll never know how hard I tried, Helen. I know some of the politicos downtown pretty well. Big shots. I tried to pull some strings, but even they couldn't get me past the damned doctors. Being Four-F, that's the worst thing that could happen to a guy."

He looked so forlorn that Helen almost reached over to touch his hand. But then she thought there was no sense in getting too friendly. This was only a temporary thing, after all.

They finished their desserts and left the two couples still sitting there.

They never did find Gregory Peck's picture on the wall.

On the way home, they listened to Glenn Miller.

"I hope you had a nice time, Helen."

"I did, Willie. I had a nice time."

"Maybe … maybe you'd like to do something like this again sometime."

There it was. She knew it was coming. "Oh, I don't think so. I sort of have someone I've been seeing."

"I didn't know that."

"Well, I do. Sort of." She'd always been a terrible liar.

"Look, Helen, I know you have lots of guys after you. And I'm not exactly the kind of guy you're used to. But, well, I've landed in some pretty good business deals. Made money, you know. I could take you to some really nice places. I don't expect anything. Just have a few laughs, is all."

Helen couldn't hide her relief that they were pulling up in front of the house. "Thanks, Willie. But I don't think so. Don't bother to get out. I can see myself to the door."

She was out of the car in a hurry and didn't turn around to wave goodbye.

The next day, MaryAnn's eyebrows were a notch higher than usual. "I can't believe you went out with Willie Churlin."

"I didn't go out with him. It was just a ride, that's all." Helen wondered why she had confided in MaryAnn in the first place.

"A midnight supper at the Starlight Terrace isn't just a ride." MaryAnn was adjusting the Venetian blinds in the apartment Papa had fixed up for her downstairs. Sunlight splashed brilliant strips over the hardwood floor.

"I'd heard about the Starlight Terrace. I wanted to see what it was like. Is that so terrible?"

"No." MaryAnn was grinning.

"I wish you'd stop smirking."

"I can't help it. I keep picturing you with Willie."

"Is it true, Helen? Did you really go out with Willie Churlin?" Bettie appeared in the doorway with a pincushion in one hand and a dress hemmer in the other.

"Well, let's just put it on the evening news, shall we?" Helen turned and flounced over to the davenport.

Bettie set the hemmer down on the floor and held out the pincushion. "I need to finish this skirt, MaryAnn. Can you mark the hem for me?"

Helen dropped to the couch and crossed one leg over the other. "I don't appreciate both of you making fun of me."

"We're not making fun." MaryAnn sat on the floor and motioned Bettie to stand in front of her. "Are you sure there's enough chalk in here, Bettie?"

"I filled it before I came down. The ruler is the right height, too. It marks the length I always wear."

Bettie squeezed the bulb and pouffed chalk onto the skirt, adding straight pins between each chalk mark. "So, what was it like, Helen?"

"What?"

"The Starlight Terrace."

Helen's eyes brightened. "The ceiling is like the evening sky, with a thousand stars winking down on you. We had lobster salad served in dishes that looked like seashells. On toast points."

"Toast points?"

"Triangles of bread with the crusts cut off," Bettie explained to MaryAnn." Mrs. Sturgill serves them with paté sometimes when she entertains."

"Paté?"

"It's a spread, MaryAnn. It comes in little cans. She showed me."

"She never showed me anything. She just kept telling me I was too slow."

"Too slow at what?"

"It didn't matter. Whatever I was doing, I was too slow."

"Mrs. Sturgill liked me."

"I think she's mean, Bettie. You found that out."

"She got me into Horace Mann."

Bettie's Graduation

Katya stood at the kitchen window and watched the dawn poke timid fingers into an overcast sky. She pulled her worn bathrobe tighter, then padded across the linoleum to the stove, poured a cup of coffee, and sat at the table. She took a long, hard pull at the liquid, grateful to get another ration of coffee this week. It was her only comfort these days, the only thing coaxing her out of bed to face another day. The news from the European front was bad; that was her daily worry. But today, she kept going over the fight with Elizabeth, picking at the scab again and again.

She'd never managed to get as close to Elizabeth—or Bettie, as she now wanted to be called—as with her other daughters, but lately, it had been getting worse. She turned up her nose at everything Katya did. Katya's clothes were out of style, and why did she wear an apron all the time, and couldn't she cut and style her hair like American mothers did? And from now on, she would be Bettie, for Bettie was not a foreign but a fresh American name.

Katya blamed the Sturgills. Although Bettie didn't work for the steel mill boss and his tony wife anymore, she had insisted on remaining at Horace Mann High School, certain graduation from that elite school would further her aim for a better life. She was still enthralled with the idea of how other people lived, like Mrs. Sturgill and her ilk and their phony airs. And last night, she'd caught Bettie sneaking around with some boy.

At seventeen, she was still too impressionable, but those days were finally over. Tonight, Bettie was graduating from high school. Monday, she'd have to find a real job.

Katya drained her coffee and heaved herself to her feet. She could hear Peter in the basement feeding wood into the little stove so they'd have hot water. He'd want breakfast. She got the eggs out of the ice box and went to get the milk from the second ice box on the back porch. Retrieving it, she vowed to get a big refrigerator right here in the kitchen as soon as the war was over. She poured a little cream from the top of the

190

milk bottle into the eggs, mixed it up, and went to put bread into the toaster.

She didn't say anything to Peter at breakfast. His asthma was bad again, and working double shifts at the mill in all that coal dust was making it worse. Bad news could bring on another attack, and she didn't want to chance it right before work. She'd tell him tonight. They'd find a way to deal with this boy.

It was after seven when Bettie came into the kitchen and poured herself a little coffee. She was wearing one of the outfits she'd made in sewing class, a white long-sleeved blouse with a pointed collar and a plaid pleated skirt.

"Ready for your last day of school? You look nice."

"Thanks. It's how everyone at school dresses."

Bettie's creed: *I believe in how everyone dresses.* Still, Katya had to admit she looked good; slim and dark-haired with those big green eyes, she was an attractive girl. And she was willing to work for what she wanted. Every penny of Sturgill's small wage had gone for fabric. She had a real talent for sewing. When she showed Katya her senior picture in the Horace Mann yearbook, she read the words underneath. "Voted Best Dressed."

"What would you like for breakfast?"

"Nothing. I'm not hungry."

"I can make you an egg. You need something in your stomach."

"You know I never like to eat this early."

Katya decided to skip their daily skirmish. At least Bettie was talking.

"There's something else," Bettie said. "I hope you're not planning to come to the graduation."

"Of course, I'm coming."

"Don't come. Please, Mama. If they find out I live outside the school boundaries, they could take away my diploma. It's not right. I've worked too hard for that."

"But to be all by yourself on such an important occasion? It's not right.
Not come to your graduation?"

"Please. I'm almost there. Don't ruin it for me."

Katya's heart sank. She should never have let her go to that fancy high school in the first place. It was Peter's boss, his wife, really, who said the girl could use their address to get into Horace Mann across town. She'd insisted the school would be better for Bettie. It would give her more opportunity, she said. Peter began to argue for it as well, and after a while, she gave in.

That night, Bettie reminded her again, "Don't ruin it, Mama. I'd die if they didn't give me my diploma. It's just a boring old ceremony, anyway, and I'll be home right after. I promise. And I'll tell you everything that happened."

But Katya went, anyway. She sat in the last row by herself and watched the well-groomed men smiling at their beautifully coiffed wives and talking with their children. Even little boys were wearing coats and ties, and the girls were in nice dresses. Except for one young man in an Air Corps uniform, there was no hint of the war in this auditorium.

Katya thought it was a dignified ceremony, and when the principal handed out the diplomas, he said Bettie had earned her degree in three years. There was an appreciative murmur from the crowd, and Katya clapped the longest in the hearty round of applause that followed. Bettie had worked hard, kept her secret for three years, and had never brought school chums home for fear they'd find out what she'd done. Katya was glad she had come to see her Elizabeth achieve the recognition she deserved.

Katya decided to try to find her afterward. She just wanted to tell her how nice she looked, tell her how proud she was that she had done what no one else in the family had ever done: graduate from high school in three years!

It took a while, but she finally spotted her, smiling and shaking hands in the vestibule and being congratulated by some of the parents. It was when Katya was starting over that she noticed him also moving toward Bettie. He was tall with dark, wavy hair, and was wearing a jacket and tie with a colored handkerchief in his breast pocket. He put a casual arm around Bettie's waist, and she was looking up at him and laughing. Then Bettie saw Katya, and the laughing stopped. Katya hesitated but then went forward, and Bettie broke away from the group.

"What are you doing here?"

"I came to tell you congratulations."

"I can't believe you did this!" She said it in a low voice and was getting two fiery spots on her cheeks. "You said you wouldn't come!"

"You have your diploma. I didn't think it would matter now."

"Of course, it matters! How could you? How could you do this to me?"

Some of the people were staring at them now, and Bettie was pulling her outside. The boy had come up, and he followed them out.

"Who is she?"

"My mother."

"Your mother?"

Katya didn't like the way he was looking her up and down with his mouth pursed. Then he held out his hand like it was some kind of present. "Harley Ashcroft."

"You're the one she's been sneaking around with?"

"I beg your pardon."

Katya wondered how he could breathe with his nostrils squeezed together like that. "How old are you?"

"I'll ... I'll be eighteen in July." For all his pretense, he was just a boy. "So, Harley Ashcroft, don't sneak around with my girl anymore. You want to see her, you come to call at the house. You sit in the front room and meet her papa. Then he'll tell you whether you can come back again."

"Listen, Mrs., um, Mrs. Cmar ..."

"No. You listen. Eliz—Bettie is seventeen. She's smart and she's got a diploma, but she's seventeen."

"Is there a problem, Harley?" A white-haired man stepped up with a look of concern on his face.

"There's no problem," Katya told him. Then, looking at Harley, she repeated, "Come to the house tomorrow at seven. We'll have some cake. And now I'm taking my girl home."

She tried talking to Bettie on the way home, telling her what she said back there was for her own good, but Bettie didn't answer. At home, she made some coffee and brought out the cake she'd made earlier as a surprise. But there was no celebration; Bettie flounced off to bed.

The next morning, she was gone.

Brindisi, Italy, 1943 - Peter Jr.'s Journal

What I remembered afterward is that the kids didn't cry. Not one—not even the babies. They just huddled together, sad-eyed pawns in the grown-up's game of life and death.

Landing at night in Yugoslavia always made us tense but tonight was worse than usual. I had flown thirty-two straight missions, and every bone in my body was crying out for reprieve. The other crewmen were just as bad. I could sense the strain in the set of Sullivan's jaw and that his big hands were tighter than usual on the yoke of our C-47 as he kept nudging the plane closer, closer to the ground. Not that the pressure was anything new. We could never be certain when we came down like this whether it would be the Yugoslav Partisans or the Krauts waiting to greet us. My radio headphones were silent. I almost missed Axis Sally purring her propaganda into my ear as we searched the mountainside for a light.

"We should be on target," Charlie, our navigator, said.

Even in the dark, I could sense the tic working in the side of Charlie's cheek the way it always did when he was under pressure. I slid forward and peered for a long time into the darkness outside the plane, my eyes burning into my head from the exertion.

We were searching for a tiny spot of light on the mountainside. At night, the Partisans would build a bonfire to mark the crude landing spot they had carved out for us somewhere in the Balkan Mountains. A fire signaled a clearing where we could drop down and unload the fresh supplies that we carried in for them. But every touch-down was a gamble all its own. One night, a line of babushkas (old women) guided us down a very treacherous dirt strip. Only their flaming torches saved us from falling into the ravine nearby. After each unloading, we would bring the wounded aboard to carry them to the safety of Allied hospitals in Italy.

"Up ahead," Sullivan said, and I spotted a fleck of light on the hillside. Breathing a sigh of relief, I watched as Sullivan eased the wheels down and headed toward the beacon.

"Nuts!" Charlie spat. And sure enough, there, further away, another dimmer light winked back at us.

"Any ideas?" Sullivan asked after a while, and together, we seemed to suck in the same deep edgy breath in the darkness. Charlie flicked his flashlight over the map again. Nobody said a word.

"Your call, Charlie."

"Gotta be the closer one."

I knew I wasn't the only one praying Charlie was right. When Krauts detected a Partisan bonfire and had enough time, they would build a fire of their own to confuse us. It had happened to other crews before us—crews that didn't come back. That's why we carried no guns anywhere on the plane. If we guessed wrong and landed in the enemy camp, Krauts were supposed to take us prisoner instead of killing us.

"If they're not our guys, I hope they've read the Geneva Convention," I said, trying to keep my voice steady.

"Don't bet your ass." Charlie's voice was soft, but it sent the blood rushing in my ears.

Sullivan gentled the yoke forward, and we dropped into the dirt. Bumping along the clearing, I tried to make out the uniforms on the shadows out there waiting for us. No luck. Herb, the flight engineer, edged toward the opening at the side of the plane. Airplane doors were a luxury reserved for peacetime, not when seconds counted as we loaded or unloaded troops in combat zones.

"Sullivan, is it you?" A guttural voice rasped out of the darkness. Then a bushy head poked its way into the plane, and I found my breath again. "You did well, my friend. I worry when I see another fire down the mountain."

"Broz. You old polecat! You know I can damn well sniff you out wherever you are."

The pockmarked face flashed a ghostly smile in Sullivan's direction. Sullivan had this way about him; he could always manage to lighten up the situation.

Quietly, we started shoving supplies off the plane into the arms of the waiting shadows. We had to work fast. We knew there were Krauts on that far mountain, but we couldn't tell what other places they might be.

Then, silently, wounded men appeared, one in the arms of a comrade while others we loaded into the plane on stretchers. There was a low groan as one stretcher bumped the side of the plane. We lifted another man inside who stared unblinking from glassy eyes. I turned away, wondering if he was dead. When the last man had been loaded, Herb signaled to Sullivan for takeoff.

"Not yet!" A woman's voice, soft but urgent, broke through the night.

She said her name was Anya, and she worked with another woman at an orphanage a few miles away.

"The Germans will be at our door any time now. Broz and his men risked their lives to warn us. Please. Could you take our children away with you, as well?"

I could hear the pleading in her voice. Sullivan looked back at the plane filled with stretchers.

"We can't take anyone else, ma'am. Too much weight. We'd never make it over the mountains."

"I only ask," she urged, "because the Germans will kill the children. That way, they don't have to feed them. In the next village, they have already killed them all.

Jesus, I muttered under my breath. *God, how I hate this war.*

I could see Sullivan's jaw working. "How many?" he wanted to know.

"Not too many." She tried to pass it off, but her voice broke. "And there is not so much weight. They're only children."

Sullivan glanced at the woman and then each one of us. Nobody looked away. He only hesitated for a moment before making up his mind. "Get 'em on board."

She turned and raised an arm above her head. After a while, I spotted them. They materialized from the trees ahead, creeping like shadowy gnomes in the moonlight. They were different ages. Older children led smaller ones by the hand; babies came in the arms of twelve-year-olds.

197

"Jesus Christ, how many are there?" Sullivan whispered as we watched the silent procession. But he made no move to stop them.

"Hurry!" he hissed as we lifted small bodies from the woman's arms into the plane. "The Krauts have given us too much time, already."

Moving the last child inside and away from the hole of a door, Herb turned toward Sullivan. An unspoken question lay between them.

"You and your friend, too!" He snapped at the woman.

"But the weight…"

"Look, they're your kids, lady. Who else will care for them if we *do* make it out of here?"

The two women clambered up, and Herb stood guard near the door. I looked around at the plane full of wounded and then at the silent children. They looked back with frightened eyes, but nobody whimpered, no one complained.

The engine cut the silence of the night as we made our way down the clearing. We taxied for a long, long time.

"Come on, baby," Sullivan urged as the plane struggled to free itself from the ground.

My throat was dry, and I closed my eyes, prodding the sluggish craft upward. Finally, with a shudder, we were airborne. But the climb was slow, and the mountains loomed ahead.

If we can just clear peak number one, I thought, *we're home free.*

For what seemed like an eternity, Sullivan inched the machine skyward. Out of the corner of my eye, I could see Charlie staring straight ahead. Herb, always the easygoing one, was rigid. Never in my life could I remember time passing so slowly.

I pinned my concentration to the moan of the engine, willing all my energy onto the power that strained to lift us skyward. Except for the engine, there was dead silence all around. The mountain was straight ahead and we weren't high enough.

"Oche nash e je yese na nebesi ...." Anya's voice was soft in my ear. I could see that her eyes were closed, her voice calm.

Suddenly, Sullivan tightened his grip and yanked hard at the yoke. I could hear the engine straining and feel the plane rise. But enough? I squeezed my eyelids together and held my breath. Forever.

"Hot damn!"

Sullivan's whoop brought me back to reality, and I looked out to see the dark shadow of the peak just below us.

"Ladies and gentlemen, boys and girls," he bellowed. "I think we just bought ourselves a ticket home!"

"Good show, captain, sir!" I cried. And I knew that I would never, ever love anybody more than I loved that big, freckled Irishman right at that moment. I turned to bask in the shy smiles on the children's faces.

"What was that you were saying back there?" I asked Anya.

"I pray," she said simply. "I pray that the children will be safe."

We made our way back to Brindisi, Italy, where we unloaded our surprising cargo. I don't know what happened to those kids after that, but I did know that they'd have a chance to grow up in a better world than the one they left behind.

Part 4:
After the War

Homecoming

"Hey, Bamboozle! I'm home … I'm home for good!"

Mari couldn't believe it. Strong arms were lifting her from behind as she was whirled around and around. Finally grounded, she turned to face her smiling brother. Johnny! Mama rushed from the kitchen, drying her hands on her apron. All three of them danced together in circles around the room. Mari didn't want to let go.

Papa came home from work. Helen and MaryAnn arrived soon after. Once again, Mama used most of the month's rationing coupons on that evening meal.

After supper, they went out on the porch to celebrate. They had endured four long years of war. Peace had been declared. Johnny had made it home.

Johnny hadn't been home for two days before Peter came. But they couldn't believe the figure turning in at the front gate belonged to the family.

"No," Mama said. "That's a Chinaman. An Oriental."

And indeed, the gaunt figure in civilian clothes hanging loose from his limbs sported skin with an unmistakably yellow pallor.

"Mom! It's me! I can't believe you don't recognize me," Peter Jr. said, coming onto the porch and dropping his duffle bag.

Then Mama flew to him and gathered him into a giant hug. "Peter! What have they done to you!"

"It's the atabrine. For my malaria. The Air Corps ran out of quinine, so they gave us all atabrine pills, which turn you yellow. And doesn't do much for malaria, either."

"You're so thin! Why are you so thin?"

"I haven't been able to eat solid food since I got back to the States. They discharged me to California. The doctor there put me back on C-rations until I could tolerate regular food again. That was weeks ago."

"Well, you're home now. It's over. Everything is fine," Mama said.

She made another fine meal, but Peter ate very little. It didn't matter. He would heal. The war was over, and they were together again. Nothing could hurt them now.

Katya said a prayer of thanksgiving that night and breathed a sigh of relief as she laid her head on her pillow. Her boys were finally home, tucked away in freshly ironed sheets in their attic bedroom. Her family was safe, and she slept, rocked into slumber by the steady rhythm of the cuckoo clock in the front room.

"Mama!"

Startled, Katya opened her eyes into darkness.

Someone was crying out in panic. Curses, followed by guttural sounds.

Katya grabbed her robe and hurried up the stairs. "Pop! Pop, you son of a gun! Pop!"

Peter was thrashing around, tangled in his sheets. Katya reached down to soothe him, only to find his bed soaking wet. A low, animal sound came from somewhere. She looked to find John cowering on the floor between the beds. Katya crossed over to turn on the lights.

Johnny sprang up, fist raised and a low, menacing sound deep in his throat.

"It's all right John," Papa said, walking into the room. "It's over."

"Pop, I say!"

"Peter! John! It's over! You're home! It's all right!"

Mama changed Peter's sheets, so wet they might have been left out in a rainstorm. Peter's nightmare had ceased, and he fell back into bed.

"What were you saying?" Papa wanted to know.

"Our missions took place at night. The Germans played "Pop Goes the Weasel," the kids' rhyme, over and over into my headphones during those raids. And you never knew how long it would take for the last line to be played. You know, 'Pop goes the weasel.' You found yourself waiting for the 'pop.' Sometimes, the wait was short. Or not. You never knew. After a while, a long wait began to mess with your mind.

"Even the nights we couldn't fly because of the weather, I would dread going to sleep. I'd hear that rhyme in my dreams. The nightmares would repeat, night after night. German mind games. Simple but very effective. They still bother me. For our part, Allies used psychological warfare, too.

"We dropped 'nickels,' or bundles of pamphlets during our raids. Some were for peaceful purposes and told the people down below where to find the food we had dropped. Others were propaganda meant to convince those in a combatant town that they were losing and should give up the fight. And all the while, the Germans had Axis Sally on the air, coaxing our boys, in her husky, come hither voice, to defect."

Both boys slept late the next morning. Finally, Mama sent Mari up to wake them. "They should eat something," she said. Johnny was on the floor again. He sprang awake with a shout. It scared Mari.

"Why does he jump up like that?" she asked Peter. "And why is he on the floor again?"

"Nights were especially dangerous for troops on the ground, Mari. Johnny was an Army Ranger. He fought many battles, and the last one was the Battle of the Bulge, a bloody battle at the end of the war. You can bet he was in a foxhole. That hole was his protection."

"War was dangerous for you, too."

"Yes, but after a raid, I flew back to our base, to the barracks, and I slept in a bed. My only regret," Peter said afterward, "was the night I didn't fly. I was bone weary and asked the commander for a night off. I always flew with an international crew, and he sent a Brit in my place. That plane never came back. I never asked for another night off."

My brother Peter flew fifty-seven straight missions, except for that one, and was awarded eight Bronze Stars and the Air Medal with two oak leaf clusters.

Peace

We slid easily into peacetime, but there were changes. The VFW (Veterans of Foreign Wars) opened a few blocks away, and the vets gathered to drink and relive their war memories. Rick said the veterans' bar kept him rooted in the war and that he wanted to move on, so he asked Papa for help in building a house.

Johnny got his first peacetime paycheck, and he bought Mama a mangle—an iron like they use in dry cleaners. It had a long roller operated with a foot pedal that lets you iron while sitting down. Ironing sheets and pillowcases was less tiring with a mangle. Like Papa said, Johnny was always looking out for Mama. Before long, Mari learned to operate the machine and took on the task of ironing the bedding.

A refrigerator went into the kitchen. No more ice box with drippy pans, but Mari would miss the iceman, the small man who swung each heavy block of ice over his shoulder with ease.

Danceland opened on the weekends, and Helen went with her friend Tillie to dance the night away. Before long, there was a tall, curly-haired boy who saw her home on the streetcar. She was smiling a whole lot these days.

Suddenly, the world was at peace, and everyone slept without the dread of the telephone summons in the dark of night.

Johnny and Peter still confronted their nightmares upstairs, but the rest of us were just grateful to have them home.

After a while, Mari grew restless. Sylvia's grandma got her a two-wheeler bike, but Mari still walked everywhere. Papa said a two-wheeler was frivolous. After a while, Edith Fleming came up with an idea.

"Here's an offer from the *Chicago Tribune* for a new two-wheeler in exchange for ten subscriptions to the newspaper. Why don't you try to sell them, Mari?"

"Why would people in Gary want to subscribe to a Chicago newspaper?"

"Because of broader news coverage and more variety. Because of gaining a wider look at the world."

So, Mari went door to door, and, to her surprise, ten people signed up, and a shiny Huffy bicycle showed up in a box on 13th Avenue. Not a Schwinn, but a wonderful blue two-wheeler that Papa put together to give her wheels.

Life went on. The same, but different. Mari still carried the war in her heart. She didn't want to, but it was there. She felt the sadness of the slaughter and the need to help figure out how to keep the world safe from bad people from now on.

And that's when she heard the bells. The war was over, and she decided to pin her hopes on an eternal good. To do good work, to honor old people and listen to what they had to say, to rejoice in the family, and to celebrate the wonders of the world around her.

Lord, help me to stand strong, even on the days I want to quit. Give me your courage when it seems easier to stop, your strong arm to hold me up when I believe I can't go on. And let me pray my thanks for life today and every day.

Acknowledgements

It takes effort to create a collection of stories. Thanks to encouragement from my grandchildren and nieces, I have written many stories. However, the task of assembling them was daunting. Kathleen McKenna, nonplused by a twelve-inch stack of stories, arranged them into this collection. Her editing and enthusiasm, coupled with Candace Scheidt's and Katy Smith's search for missing historical facts, brought the story together. Jenny Kalahar's thoughtful recommendations and editing polished the stories further for publication. I am also grateful to my daughter, Mary Lou Cox, and her family for their encouragement, technical assistance and determination to help me share these stories with others.

Made in the USA
Monee, IL
06 July 2025

20459803R00132